A MAN PURSUED

After two years in prison, Matt Sutton thought the fifty thousand dollars he'd buried would buy a new life with beautiful, blonde gambler Diana Logan. Unfortunately, he was a target for everybody who wanted to get rich quick, not forgetting his old cellmate Cole Devlin and his outlaw gang. Worse still, he hadn't counted on Devlin taking Diana hostage. But Matt was determined to have both the money and his girl, and his six-gun would deal death to all who got in his way.

Books by James Gordon White
in the Linford Western Library:

COMANCHE CAPTIVE
RHONE

JAMES GORDON WHITE

◆──────────────◆

A MAN
PURSUED

Complete and Unabridged

LINFORD
Leicester

First published in Great Britain in 1998 by
Robert Hale Limited, London

First Linford Edition
published 1999
by arrangement with
Robert Hale Limited, London

British Library CIP Data

White, James Gordon
  A man pursued.—Large print ed.—
  Linford western library
  1. Western stories
  2. Large type books
  I. Title
  813.5'4 [F]

  ISBN 0–7089–5567–3

Published by
F. A. Thorpe (Publishing) Ltd.
Anstey, Leicestershire

Set by Words & Graphics Ltd.
Anstey, Leicestershire
Printed and bound in Great Britain by
T. J. International Ltd., Padstow, Cornwall

To
my wife, Marie,
and James Sr. & Solveig

1

Moving with surprising speed for his size, the big man fired and broke cover, heading for an outcropping of rocks diagonally above on the mountainside.

He almost made it.

A blood-spurting hole appeared in the left side of his chest before the flat crack of a carbine reached his ears. He grunted deeply, half-twisting around with the bullet's impact, and fell backward, rolling head over heels with the loose-limbed ease of a circus acrobat. A shower of dirt and rocks followed him down the mountainside. He jarringly came to rest with his back against a huge rock, his glazed eyes staring up at the already blazing, mid-morning Arizona sun.

From a broad ledge high above, Matt Sutton grimly ejected the spent shell from his carbine. Grey eyes, slitted beneath the wide brim of his flatcrowned hat, swept the area below.

There had been three of them on his trail for over a week, since his release from Yuma Territorial Prison. One of them was an expert tracker. Every time he thought he'd given them the slip, they'd shown up a few hours later, just like bad pennies. Finally, he'd had enough; he was too near his destination to be fretting about them any longer. He'd challenged them, they'd answered with gunshots, and the fight was on. He'd shortened the odds, but there were two more skulking down below.

The jaw muscles of Matt's lean, hard-boned face clenched as a bullet whizzed past his right ear. Then he heard the shot and saw its puff of smoke from a crevice between two huge rocks. The fool had boxed himself in good. Well, he'd deal with him now, before he realized his perilous situation, and worry about the third man later.

Raising his rifle, Matt began firing rapidly. The slugs whined like a swarm of angry bees, ricocheting about madly inside the crevice. The man's echoing terrified yelps quickly became high-pitched screams of anguish as Matt continued pumping slugs into the crevice. The screams abruptly stopped, but Matt didn't quit firing until his rifle clicked empty.

The crack of the last shot drifted off into the still desert air and there was only silence. Then a stirring came from inside the crevice . . . and out lurched a walking dead man, his shirt and pants blood-soaked. His arm attempted to raise his pistol, but the effort was too great. Suddenly he pitched forward, firing into the dirt, and landed face down. His body spasmed, then was motionless.

As Matt hastily started to reload, he heard movement behind him and spun. A fist crashed into the side of his jaw, knocking his hat off and hurling him around to collide with the large rock that had sheltered him from the men below. The carbine and shells fell from his hands as he began a downward slide. The ham-like hands of the brawny, thick-necked man who towered over him caught his shirt front and yanked him up again, bracing him against the rock. Matt's hand weakly clawed at the gun in his holster. Before he could clear leather, a swipe of the man's huge paw sent the six-gun flying from his grasp. The man released him and, grinning savagely, slowly drew back a big fist.

Dazed as he was, Matt lowered his head and, shoving with a foot against the rock, launched himself at the man's protruding belly. He heard the air whoosh out of the big man's lungs and felt the blow intended for his face strike down on the middle of his back with only half its force. Then they hit the ground and rolled about in a twisting, tumbling knot of madly flailing arms and legs.

The big man hurled Matt away, gained his feet and, rushing him, aimed a powerful kick at his head that would have brought the fight to an abrupt end then and there. Matt rolled into the man's other leg, slammed the heel of his palm into his opponent's kneecap and knocked him sprawling.

Matt staggered to his feet and shook his head to clear it. The delay cost him the momentary advantage he held, but he was in no condition to follow through. The big man was on his feet and coming at him.

They circled, feinting, weaving, dodging, swinging punches that either missed, or did slight damage. In his twenty-eight years, Matt Sutton had had more than his share of fights and, to his credit, he'd won far more than he'd lost. In prison you couldn't afford to lose, and this fight was no different. Though tall, lean and broad-shouldered, he was a good two inches shorter and over thirty pounds lighter than the other man, whom he recognized as Clyde Cleehan, an inmate who'd been released a week before him.

'Cut me in, Sutton,' the big man growled, 'and I won't break your back.'

'You're at a disadvantage, Cleehan,' Matt said between breaths. He side-stepped a wild swing, hooked a short, vicious blow to the big man's ribs, then danced back and continued, 'You can't risk killing me, but I've got no concern about killing you.' He suddenly sprang forward with the speed of a cat and clubbed a fist against the man's left ear.

The impact rocked Cleehan's head to his shoulder, and he backed away, swaying unsteadily on his feet. 'I'll pound you till you talk,' he threatened gruffly.

As though by mutual agreement, the men drew back and stood, lungs heaving, raking each other with their eyes. 'That's been tried before,' Matt said, grinning mirthlessly. 'But a beating is no good without the threat of death behind it. And, in this case, if I talk I'm a dead man.'

'I ain't gonna kill you, Sutton,'

Cleehan said, far too quickly. 'All I'm askin' for is half.'

'Go to hell,' Matt said softly, without emotion.

'By damn, you'll talk before I'm through!' the big man said, his pig eyes mean and narrow, and hurled himself at Matt.

Matt met his charge with a hard left, followed by a right. Muscles rippling across his shoulders, he felt the impact right down to his boots as the blow connected solidly with Cleehan's chin and bone crunched against bone. The big man stumbled, went to one knee. Matt drove a fist down at him. Cleehan tried to dodge, but Matt's fists crashed against his temple. As Cleehan fell forward his arms snaked around Matt's legs, dragging him to the dirt with him.

They rolled across the ground and came to a stop with Cleehan on top, straddling and choking Matt, whose head hung over the edge of the cliff. Matt winced at the blinding pain as

Cleehan's thick fingers dug into his throat, cutting off his breath. His vision blurred, his lungs felt close to bursting.

Summoning his last bit of waning strength, Matt brought his arms up inside Cleehan's and smashed them apart, breaking his crushing grip. His body bucked and he brought his knees up hard against the big man's back.

With a surprised roar that fast became a terrified scream, Cleehan was pitched forward over Matt's head and out into thin air. Matt rolled over and stared down after him.

Flapping like a scarecrow in a wind storm, Cleehan's screaming body twisted and turned in the air as it plummeted toward the rocks far below. The screams came to an abrupt end when he crashed down on top of a huge rock and lay awkwardly, spreadeagled upside down, a bright red stream oozing out from the back of his crushed skull.

Matt stared down impassively at the dead man whose wide, glazed eyes seemed to stare back malevolently. Then he shoved himself to his feet, dusted his clothes and, every muscle in his long frame aching, slowly walked away.

★ ★ ★

It was well past noon when Matt Sutton topped a barren hill and saw the town of Bedlow spread out before him. Things had sure changed in a little over two years. With the arrival of the railroad, the town had become a shipping point for ranchers and, eager to milk the miners and cowboys in that part of the territory, individual merchants and saloon-keepers had hastily thrown up a sprawl of rough board buildings. Except for the main street, which ran straight through town, the others appeared to be no more than twisting, cross-angled paths winding through jumbled clusters of low buildings. On the far side of town stood the stock pens, crowded with cattle ready for shipping, and a few livery stables.

Matt sat his sorrel and stared reflectively at the town. He'd be about as welcome as a fox in a hen house, but his girl was down there and he wanted to see her before he tended to his other business. She was the only good thing to ever come into his life. She'd stuck by him when he'd been sent to prison. Her letters and the few brief visits they'd been allowed had helped him to keep his sanity in that hell-hole. Now that he was out they'd never be parted again.

As Matt continued staring at the town, he thought about the events in his life that had led him here. His parents and older brother had been butchered on their West Texas ranch by an Apache raiding party while he, aged six, had cowered in a hidden pit behind the house.

The next day a neighbouring family had found him and taken him in, but they already had a son, so his lot was to become a cheap hired hand. Life was tolerable until Mrs Marsh died when he was thirteen. A week later he ran away.

From then on he was a drifter, working at any odd job he could get. He washed dishes, cleaned cuspidors in a saloon, worked in a livery stable, and then went back to punching cattle. That was when he met Jake Caskie.

Jake was five years older, but just as wild. They drank, brawled and whored together, and succeeded in getting themselves fired from one ranch after another. It was while they were lying over in Bedlow that Matt met Diana Logan and started thinking about growing up and assuming responsibilities. Unfortunately, Caskie convinced him to go along with one last high-spirited escapade.

They robbed a stagecoach, and the $50,000 in the strongbox surprised even them. For two days they kept ahead of the posse, then their luck ran out. Trapped, they shot it out until Jake was killed, and Matt took

11

a bullet through his right shoulder.

Throughout his trial he stoutly maintained that Caskie had hidden the money and taken the secret with him. Nobody believed him. He was sentenced to five years in prison. Good behaviour, plus saving the warden from a crazed, knife-wielding prisoner, got him released in two years.

Matt's thin lips curled in a grin and he rubbed a hand over his stubbled cheeks. Two years of his life in exchange for $50,000 might not sound like such a bad deal to some, but he'd earned every penny of it in that stinking prison — and now he was going to collect.

He nudged a booted heel against his horse's ribs and started down the hill.

★ ★ ★

The streets of Bedlow were already starting to crowd up with raucous cowboys and miners with loose money to spend, and most took no notice

12

of the tall stranger in the faded blue shirt and kerchief and shotgun chaps, his dove-grey, flat-crowned hat set at a rakish angle. Before he'd ridden three blocks along the urine and manure-spotted main street, some of the more respectable and permanent citizens recognized him and uneasy stares and murmurs spread like wildfire along the boardwalks.

Deputy Billy Clark sat with his chair propped back on two legs against the wall of the sheriff's office. Stocky, bandy-legged, with red hair and accompanying freckles, he'd been a brash lad of eighteen when Matt Sutton had been sent to prison. Two years and a deputy's badge hadn't improved Billy Clark's manners. He strutted the streets of Bedlow like a bantam rooster, bullying anybody he could.

The sight of Matt Sutton leisurely riding past brought Clark up with a start and he almost tipped over his chair in his haste to get out of it. An ex-outlaw was fair game, and if he could

13

buffalo Sutton the whole town would look up to him. Sutton's speed with a gun had never been determined, but either way he'd been without practice for over two years. Billy Clark had been practising his fast draw every day and, while he'd never been in a gunfight, he knew that he was damn good.

Hitching up his double-holstered gunbelt, he was about to start after Sutton when the front door opened and Sheriff Keeler stepped out of his office. 'Sheriff . . . ' Clark began.

'I seen him,' Keeler said, his voice utterly cold as he tucked his familiar shotgun under his arm. He was followed out by Yance Boyne, a slim, wiry man several years older than Billy, who carried a Winchester and was everything a deputy should be that Billy was not.

At the sight of the two men, Billy Clark's hopes of glory fell. Keeler's stern, weather beaten face made it clear that he would deal with Sutton his own way. Trying to hide his disappointment,

Billy reluctantly allowed Keeler to take the lead and, putting on his best solemn expression, fell in behind with Yance. As they clomped along the boardwalk, people cleared a wide path for them. That was as it should be thought Billy, dreaming of the day when folks would give him a wide berth whenever he marched around town.

Matt Sutton reined in his horse before the Cut and Shoot Saloon and sat staring at its red and gold elaborately scrolled sign. The building's façade was like its interior: big, proud and gaudy. The saloon would have seemed more at home in St Louis or San Francisco's notorious Barbary Coast than in the small town of Bedlow. But as customers stoutly believed 'what's biggest is best' the Cut and Shoot had no real competition from the three or four other saloon-gambling halls in town.

During one of her prison visits the year before, Diana had told him about an enterprising gambler from Kansas City who'd tried to erect a rival palace, only to have it mysteriously burn down the night before it opened. The man had accused Jack Rath, the proprietor of the Cut and Shoot, but no solid evidence could be found to link him to the most welcome burning. A week later, the gambler had been gunned down from a dark alley while on his way to his hotel with his night's winnings. Naturally, Rath and his bullies all had unshakeable alibis. Since that night nobody had been foolish enough to seriously challenge the Cut and Shoot's supremacy.

Ignoring the small, gawking crowd that had gathered on the boardwalk, Matt loosely swung from the saddle, tied the reins to a hitching rail and moved to the three steps leading up to the saloon's swinging half doors.

As he was about to mount the second step, a hard voice called, 'Hold it, Sutton!'

Recognizing the voice, Matt turned very slowly and was careful to keep his hand away from his six-gun. A shooting was the last thing he wanted.

Sheriff Harry Keeler, double-barrelled shotgun held ready, strode down the middle of the street with two deputies, both less than half his age, trailing behind and to either side of him. Tall, heavy-set, hatchet-faced, with salt and pepper hair and drooping handlebar moustache, Keeler was a formidable lawman. Though past fifty, the years had not sapped his vigour. His frame was still ramrod straight and in his sober black suit, string tie and high-crowned hat he still looked every bit his nickname: the undertaker.

'I'm a free man now, Keeler,' Matt said easily, as the three men came up and stopped about a dozen feet from him.

The sheriff nodded tensely. 'So I heard, and I been expectin' you.'

Matt's gaze roamed from Keeler's steely-blue eyes to the deputies, both coiled springs, and then slowly back, a hint of amusement briefly playing across his face; the undertaker sure wasn't taking any chances. 'I'm not spoiling for a fight,' he said flatly. 'You know why I'm here — and my business don't include you.' He started to turn away. 'Now, if I haven't broken any laws . . . '

'You're wearin' a gun.'

Matt frowned. 'I didn't see any firearms ordinance posted at the town limit.'

'It's my own law,' Keeler informed him, 'for special visitors like you.' His cold blue eyes met Matt's. 'If you want to stay in town, hand over your gun.'

Matt set his jaw and measured Keeler. This was an unexpected dilemma. He didn't cotton one bit to the idea of walking around Bedlow unarmed, not after his run-in with Cleehan and his partners. Behind him, a hush had fallen over the onlookers and a multitude of footsteps were heard urgently retreating away from what, at any moment, might be the line of fire.

A deadly silence hung in the air. Time seemed suspended. Matt saw the taut dark skin over Keeler's prominent cheekbones twitch, saw the young frecklefaced deputy's stubby fingers hover above his twin guns, saw the taller deputy, Winchester ready, tensely waiting for his movement to begin firing.

'What's it to be, Sutton?' Keeler asked, his voice low and sharp.

Slowly a cold smile spread over Matt's face. He was too close to his goal to let his pride get him gunned down now. Let the fools talk about how the undertaker and his deputies had backed Matt Sutton down. 'All right, Keeler,' he said easily, 'you can have it.'

Not relaxing a muscle, Keeler said, 'Take off the gunbelt slow'n easy — with your left hand.' Matt carefully obeyed and held out the gunbelt. Keeler still didn't relax; he'd been a lawman too long to be taken in by an apparently unarmed man. 'Toss it to the deputy,' he commanded, giving a slight nod to Billy Clark. Matt tossed the gunbelt to the redheaded youth who made no attempt to catch it and smirked cockily as it landed in the dirt before him. Matt eyed him narrowly, but kept his anger in check. 'Git his rifle, too, Clark,' Keeler ordered.

Almost as one the spectators sighed their relief, awed by Keeler's bloodless victory. There were also a few disappointed murmurs from those who were all set to watch somebody die. Clark scooped up the gunbelt, slung it over a shoulder, then strutted to Matt's sorrel and jerked the carbine from its saddle holster.

'You can pick up your weapons on your way out of town — at sundown,' Keeler said pointedly.

'I don't plan on leaving that soon.'

'I'm makin' an allowance by lettin' you stay that long!'

'And I've made an allowance by letting you have my guns.'

'I don't want you in *my* town,' Keeler said, his face like iron.

'I'll be responsible for Mr Sutton's

actions, Sheriff Keeler,' a deep, good-natured voice said, breaking the tension. Matt shifted his eyes from Keeler and saw Lew Gillum approaching. The husky, middle-aged man in a derby and yellow checked suit strode up and placed himself between Matt and Keeler. His face was open and friendly and a mite jowly.

'I don't know, Mr Gillum,' Keeler said, frowning.

'My company will appreciate your co-operation,' cajoled Gillum with a wink and a nod.

Keeler considered, then nodded grudgingly. 'Awright, he can stay for a while. But you'n me got some talkin' to do, Mr Gillum.'

'Fine,' Gillum said, smiling and nodding as though he'd just been asked to Sunday dinner. 'I'll see you in your office shortly.' Keeler turned on his heel and stalked away, followed by Yance. Billy Clark delayed to give Matt a taunting grin, then turned and, puffing out his chest, ambled after Keeler.

Matt watched the departing men with an amused smile then turned to Gillum who walked up and extended his hand. He hesitated, staring at Gillum's hand, then took it. 'Never thought I'd see the day when a Pinkerton man would be stickin' up for me,' he said dryly.

'Why not,' Gillum said pleasantly, 'my company has an interest in you.'

'They have a long memory.'

'They never give up until they get what they're after.'

Matt shook his head. 'My story's still the same as it was two years ago.'

'I've been authorized to tell you that there's a ten per cent recovery fee for that money — no questions asked.' He paused, eyeing Matt evenly for a moment, then added, 'Five thousand's a lot of money.'

'Fifty thousand's a whole lot more — *if* I did know where it was.'

Gillum shrugged. 'Sometimes it's smart to settle for second best. Right now you're a target for anybody who wants to get rich quick. They're going to come swarming on you like bees to honey, and you're going to wish you were back in that nice, safe prison cell.'

'Three fellas already had that idea,' Matt said tonelessly. 'Turned out to be fatal for them.'

'See; it's already started.'

'I appreciate your concern,' Matt said dryly, 'but I can take care of myself.'

'But for how long?' Gillum asked. Matt shrugged and started to turn away. 'Oh, by the way,' Gillum said, 'your friend Cole Devlin has a new gang and is rumoured to be operating around here.'

Matt scowled at the mention of Devlin's name and the memories it invoked. 'Just because we shared the same cell for over a year, that don't make us friends.'

'Either way, I'm sure he doesn't believe your story any more than my company does.'

'That's his problem.'

Gillum smiled pleasantly. 'I just thought I'd do you a favour by letting you know he's in these parts.'

'Now if you really want to do me a favour,' Matt said, returning Gillum's smile, 'you can check my horse at the livery stable.' He paused, then added pointedly, 'I won't be needing him for a while.'

'Happy to oblige,' Gillum said, retaining his smile. 'I'll put him in Turner's, that's the one I'm using.'

'Thanks. That'll be real cosy,' Matt said mirthlessly. 'Be seeing you, Gillum.'

'You can count on that, Matt.'

Matt was aware of Gillum's eyes following him up the steps and to the saloon's batwing doors. He dismissed the Pinkerton man from his mind and pushed through the swinging doors into the cool interior of the barn-like saloon.

2

Matt stood surveying the huge room. It was still early and the gaming-tables stood empty. A fat piano player, in shirtsleeves and fancy garter, half-heartedly plunked out a tune near the curtained concert stage dominating the far side of the room. The gaudily clad saloon girls well outnumbered the handful of customers scattered about at tables and the long, highly polished mahogany bar, with its huge pickle jar and free lunch display. A brawny, bearded hardcase lounged indolently beside the stairs leading to the private rooms above, which included Jack Rath's living-quarters and those of his privileged few.

Matt's face lit up as his sweeping gaze settled on a table by a stained-glass window where a young, weakly handsome man in a yellow silk shirt and bright red kerchief sat talking with a slender, golden-haired woman with milk-white skin. Though her back was to him, Matt was certain she was Diana. Grinning widely, he started forward.

The young man paled as he saw Matt coming and spoke to the woman. She turned and watched him with large, curious, brown eyes. Matt's spirits immediately fell.

She was *not* Diana.

She was about nineteen. Her beautiful, delicate features, marred only by a shade too much paint and powder, were close enough for her to pass as Diana's younger sister.

But Diana Logan didn't have a younger sister. As Matt self-consciously veered away from the table, a cheerful voice called his name from above. He turned and saw Jack Rath coming down the stairs with his ever-present shadow, Rio, a lean, stoic gunman whose pale eyes and almost colourless lashes intimidated those around him.

'H'lo, Jack,' Matt said casually, and ambled toward the stairs. The bearded tough at the bottom of the stairs drew himself erect and glared at Matt with hard, pig eyes.

'It's all right, Norton,' the saloon keeper said, reaching the bottom step and moving forward to meet Matt. 'Mr Sutton and I are old friends.' The bearded man relaxed, but continued eyeing Matt sullenly. Matt ignored both him and Rio and shook hands with Rath. 'You're looking fit, Matt,' Rath remarked, and plunged his thumbs into the pockets of his fancy gold vest, adorned with a long gold watch fob.

Matt took in Rath's expensive, tailored black suit and diamond stick pin. 'And you're looking prosperous as ever.'

Rath's broad face broke into an easy smile and he stroked his thin moustache which, like his temples and long dark sideburns, showed signs of grey. At forty-five, he still looked a good ten years younger and his tall frame was hard and muscular. 'Business has been good lately.'

'When aren't the odds always with the house?' Matt asked dryly, remembering the card sharps and rigged gaming-tables.

'There have been 'rare' occasions,' Rath said good-naturedly, choosing to ignore his subtle jibe, 'luckily, not *too* often. But you're not here to gamble, are you?'

'Getting from one day to the next is a gamble.'

Rath nodded and gestured toward the stairs. 'She's up there. Second door on the left.'

'Thanks.'

'I took the liberty of telling her you were here.' A hint of annoyance played across Matt's face; he was hoping to surprise Diana. Rath clapped him on the shoulder and gave him a false, friendly smile. 'Women like a little notice so they can look their best.'

Matt nodded and returned Rath's false smile. 'That was real considerate,

Jack . . . I gotta remember not to tell you any secrets.' He strode to the stairs and started up.

Rath stared after Matt, then turned to Rio. 'Pass the word to the boys. I want them to keep an eye on Sutton without being obvious about it. He won't try for that money right away, but sooner or later he will and we'll be ready.' Rio nodded and headed for the door and Rath leisurely made his way to the bar.

As Rio stalked past their table Jenny Taylor and the young man in the bright yellow silk shirt abruptly broke off their low conversation. After the gunman had gone, Emmet Wade said tensely, 'Cole has to know about Sutton,' and pushed back his chair.

'But Emmet . . . ' Jenny began, leaning forward and catching his hand.

He hesitated, frowning. 'Do you have somethin' against being rich?'

She shook her head and answered meekly, 'Not if you want us to be.'

Emmet patted her hand and flashed

a confident grin. 'That's exactly what I want for us, Jenny.' He stood, pulled his dusty Stetson low on his shaggy brown head, and announced, 'I'll be back later.'

Jenny nodded, forced a smile and watched him leave. Every time they parted she fretted about seeing him again. For almost six months now, Emmet had been riding with the Devlin gang, and his boastful stories of their minor exploits constantly raised fears for his safety. From what she'd heard about Matt Sutton he wasn't one to be stirred up — and that was just what Cole Devlin and his bunch had in mind.

A drummer with thick greasy hair and a round, sweaty face intruded on her thoughts. Jenny wanted to send him away but Rath was at the bar. She mustered her most enticing smile and agreed to have a drink with him. Talking was better than sitting and troubling herself about Emmet. Still, for the first time in the eight months she'd worked here, she found herself wishing that her drink was real whiskey, instead of the lukewarm tea all of the girls were served.

* * *

At his knock, the door instantly flew open and, after more than two years, Matt Sutton finally found himself standing before Diana Logan without any hindering prison bars or wire-mesh screens between them. She was even more exquisite than he remembered.

Her face was a lovely ivory cameo, with big startling blue eyes, high cheekbones and red, finely moulded lips. Honey-gold hair cascaded well below her slim, straight shoulders. At twenty-six, she didn't look much more than twenty.

She spoke his name softly. Matt stepped into the room. She closed and locked the door, then turned to him, her face radiant. In her French-heeled bedroom slippers she was almost his eye level. A white silk robe, tightly belted to accentuate her narrow waist, seductively hugged her slender, magnificent form and boldly outlined the swell of her high, firm bosom, rising with every breath.

His own breath tight in his chest, Matt reached for her hesitantly, afraid she would disappear at his touch.

She didn't.

Taking her shoulders, he stiffly lowered his face to hers and kissed her gently, almost reverently. She didn't move, just stood there, head back, eyes closed, letting him taste her soft, moist lips.

Then she thrust against him, opening her mouth wide under his with a low moan, her lips moving in small, desperate circles. He felt her breasts pressing into his shirt, felt her thighs against his, and was aware of the heat sweeping through his veins like a prairie fire.

Whether the kiss lasted for minutes or hours, neither knew nor cared.

Then, slowly, with reluctance, Diana's parted lips slid off his. She tilted her blonde head back, her red mouth glistening, and looked lovingly up into his face. 'Matt, it's been so long . . . ' she sighed, her velvet voice husky with emotion.

'Too damn long . . . ' he agreed, holding her close, luxuriating in the feel of her supple body and the delicate fragrance of her perfume.

'You should have told me when you'd be here.'

'I had no idea, Diana,' he said honestly. 'But I did know nothing was going to get in my way.' Gently he disengaged himself, drew her back at arm's length and looked her up and down, very slowly and admiringly, as though impressing every inch of her in his mind. The lower part of her robe had parted, exposing one long, lovely, satin-smooth leg and its trim, precise ankle.

She glanced down at her robe. 'I wanted to dress especially for you,' she said self-consciously, 'but there wasn't enough time to decide — '

'You'd look beautiful in rags,' Matt interrupted softly. Smiling, she glided forward into his embrace, once more pressing her softness against him from shoulder to legs. Her lips burned briefly on his, then she put her cheek on his chest. Matt stared over the top of her pale head at the open doorway leading into her bedroom, then swept her up in his arms; a slipper fell from one shapely bare foot and thudded on the carpet. Diana shook off its mate and draped her arms about his neck as Matt strode to the bedroom.

* * *

Emmet Wade wound his way up a mountain trail between a tangle of rocks and stunted pine. He'd travelled the trail often enough that he could afford to let his mind drift and rely on his horse to find its own way to Cole Devlin's hide-out. To a 19-year-old who'd run away from the drudgery of a Kansas farm falling in with an outlaw bunch was an exciting life. And being their eyes and ears in Bedlow filled him with self-importance.

It was an easy job, made even easier last month when Cole Devlin had decided to halt operations and wait for Matt Sutton's arrival. With $50,000 at stake, it didn't make good sense to chance getting shot up or arrested pulling a job for less money. Also, if the law got too riled up it wouldn't be safe in these parts. And it was important to be around Bedlow when Sutton came for his woman. Once the two of them had gone it would surely be a chore to find them again.

Emmet's thoughts turned to what he'd do with his share of all that money. Jenny was always talking about going East and starting a new life. Well, they could give it a try, and then go some place else if they didn't like it. That was the pleasurable thing about having money, being able to do whatever you felt like doing. The sooner Cole heard about Sutton, the sooner they'd all be spending that money.

Emmet kicked the brown gelding into a faster pace, and a mile and a half later rounded a bend and approached a distant clearing where an old cabin and ramshackle barn stood, fighting a losing battle with the elements. There was a sudden rustling in the bushes ahead on the left side of the trail, and an ugly, bearded giant, in jeans, leather vest and flannel shirt, all well worn, lumbered out onto the trail, lowering a Winchester. Emmet reined in his panting horse.

'Well now,' sneered the man known only as Shank, 'who's a-chasin' you?'

'Where's Cole?' Emmet asked excitedly.

Before the big man could respond, Jesse Hayne pushed through the bushes. Lean, wiry, grizzled, Jesse looked and dressed exactly what he was: a middle-aged cowhand who'd come upon hard times. 'He's back at the cabin,' Jesse drawled. 'But I'd wait a spell if I was you, boy.'

'This won't keep,' Emmet said, and heeled his horse past the men.

'Maybe one of us shoulda tole him Cole's busy with Rose,' Jesse commented dryly. Shank gave an uninterested shrug and walked away.

★ ★ ★

Shoving his straight, greasy black hair out of his long, gaunt, homely face with both hands, Cole Devlin stood smiling down at Rose, squirming enticingly on the bunk. The beautiful half-breed was like a sly, untamed critter.

A tangled mass of flowing, midnight-black hair partly hid her lovely face, emphasizing her sharp, prominent high cheekbones and strong, clean-cut jawline. Her full, pouting mouth, wide nostrils and slim, black brows, arched over dark, challenging eyes, added to her aura of sensuality. She lay there panting and purring like a big cat with that sassy 'are you man enough?' look. The point of her tongue crept out and briefly licked at her wet, ripe lips while her slim fingers trailed over her firm, copper-skinned body.

A lustful desire burning in him, Cole started unbuttoning his red long johns. He was almost out of them when Emmet Wade's excited voice shouted his name and footsteps raced to the back-room door. Rose gave a startled cry and snatched the rumpled bedcovers to hide her nakedness. No sooner did Cole struggle back into his long johns than Emmet burst in. He saw them, halted dead in mid-stride, and his face became almost crimson beneath its tan.

'Emmet, what the hell,' Cole roared, clasping his unfastened long johns together in front of him like a modest young girl. 'Can't a body ever git a little peace!'

'I . . . I'm sorry, Cole,' Emmet muttered, averting his eyes to the floor and fidgeting sheepishly.

'I'll say you are,' Cole snapped. 'Now git on outa here!'

'But — ' Emmet began, jerking his eyes from the floor.

'If'n I hafta go over there to you,' Cole interrupted harshly, 'I'm gonna thump you good.'

'Matt Sutton's at the saloon!' Emmet blurted, retreating into the doorway. He saw Devlin hesitate, the anger leaving his cloudy face, and quickly pressed on. 'And he ain't got his guns. Sheriff Keeler made him give 'em up while he's in town.'

Cole eyed him dubiously. 'That sure don't sound like Sutton . . . '

'Me and half the town saw him do it.'

A cunning smile stole over Cole's face. 'Now it's gonna be just like takin' candy from a baby.' He gave a broad wave. 'Go tell the others to start gittin' ready. I'll be there directly.' Emmet spun and went out, slamming the door. Cole hastily did up his long johns and began gathering his strewn clothes from the floor.

'Cole-honey,' Rose whined seductively, emerging from beneath the bedcovers, 'we ain't even started.' She was unable to see his pained look as he raised his eyes to the ceiling and sighed.

'There'll be plenty of time after me and the boys git back with Sutton's woman.'

Rose's dark eyebrows knitted in a scowl. 'I don't see why you hafta bring her here . . . '

Cole slipped on his pants. 'I done tole you he'll do anythin' for that woman,' he said patiently. 'And he'll part with that money just to git her back.'

'Is she pretty?' Rose asked suspiciously.

' 'Course she is. He ain't gonna give away fifty thousand dollars for no ugly woman.'

'Is she prettier 'n me?' Rose probed.

Cole wisely evaded the question with a question. 'Are you gittin' jealous on me, Rose-honey?'

'You even look cross-eyed at another

40

woman, and I'll cut her up!' Rose flared.

'Well, don't go cuttin' on this one,' Cole said, putting on his shirt. 'She's business and that's all.'

'She better be,' Rose warned. 'You're *my* man, Cole.'

'I know that,' Cole agreed, and flashed his very best ingratiating smile. 'You're the one who seems to be forgittin'.' He moved to the bunk, sat heavily, and began pulling on his boots.

Softening, Rose meekly scooted to his side. 'I'm sorry, Cole,' she purred, nuzzling his cheek. 'It's just I love you so much. I'd do anythin' for you, you know that.'

Cole stamped on a boot and turned to her. 'And that's how it oughta be.' He brushed a stream of raven hair away from her face and over her shoulder. 'You just mind yourself around Sutton's woman,' he said pleasantly, almost as if to a child, 'and by tomorrow night we'll be on

41

our way to Mexico with fifty thousand Yankee greenbacks in our poke.'

'I can hardly wait!' cried Rose, hugging him happily.

Cole held her nakedness to him, but his mind was on Matt Sutton's beautiful, blonde hunk of woman.

3

After leaving Matt Sutton's horse at
Turner's, with orders to the stableman
to send him immediate word if Sutton
took the horse out, Lew Gillum had
gone to the jailhouse and extracted
a promise from Sheriff Keeler not to
harass Sutton. That snot-nose punk
deputy Billy Clark troubled him, but
it was Keeler's job to keep a tight rein
on him. Otherwise, he would personally
take the little pest into a back alley and
cripple him, by God!

Fully dressed, Gillum now lay on
his hotel bed trying to shut out the
late-afternoon street sounds and nap.
Starting tonight he was going to keep
an eye on the livery stable. It might
be too soon, but you never could tell.
After being with his girl all day Sutton
might get restless and figure no one
would expect him to go for the money

this early. If not, it would mean a lot of sleepless nights, but that was nothing new to the Pinkerton man.

Gillum closed his eyes and began counting to $50,000, very slowly. In no time at all he fell asleep, a contented smile upon his face.

★ ★ ★

It was early evening, and the Cut and Shoot Saloon's customers were straggling in after their suppers in twos and threes. Emmet Wade and Jenny Taylor sat talking together in low voices at a secluded table, pausing whenever a customer or saloon girl passed near.

'I mean it, Emmet,' Jenny said nervously, after hearing Cole Devlin's plan. 'I have a bad feeling about all this.'

'Jenny, there's nothing to worry about. Cole has everything figured. You just get Sutton's girl to go outside with you, and Cole will do the rest.'

'I . . . I just hate to do it,' Jenny

said guiltily. 'Diana has been so nice to me. Isn't there another way?'

'They're not going to hurt her. She'll be right back here by tomorrow night.'

'You're sure?'

'That's what Cole said.' Jenny's expression made it plain that Cole Devlin's word inspired no confidence. Emmet leaned closer, took her hand in both of his, and said earnestly, 'When I get my share of that money, we're on our own. We'll go back East, or any place you want, and live like nice respectable folks.'

'Oh, Emmet!' Jenny cried, and covered his face with little kisses.

'Then you'll do your part?'

Jenny nodded. She banished her guilty conscience by once more dreaming of lovely homes on treelined streets, of quiet Sunday walks with civilized folk who didn't carry guns, and of theatres, parties, and having real friends, and all the other wonderful fantasies so dear to an orphan girl from New Mexico Territory.

They'd eaten a leisurely supper in Diana's room and were relaxing on her large comfortable bed. Matt's arm was around Diana as she snuggled contentedly against him, her head resting on his muscular chest, her long honey-gold hair fanned out over her face.

Diana sighed from beneath her hair. 'I should be downstairs dealing faro,' she said, without enthusiasm.

'You worried Rath will fire you?'

She gave a small shrug. 'He might.'

Matt shook his head. 'Not till he gets his hands on my money.'

Diana raised her head. 'Jack has enough money.'

'Nobody ever has enough money. Why do you think he put you up in this fancy place — because you're a good faro dealer?'

'The customers seem to think so,' she answered lightly.

'He's like Gillum and all the rest,

46

just waiting for me to make a move toward the money.'

'Are you?'

'When the time's right.'

Diana drew her long legs under her and sat up over him. 'Matt, it's only going to bring more trouble. Leave it, and we'll go somewhere and start new.'

'That money's mine,' Matt said firmly. 'I bought and paid for it with over two years in a stinking hellhole.'

'You're back now. And I want to keep you — with or without the money. Matt, I've heard there are all sorts of opportunities in California.'

'Sure, but we need a grubstake. It takes money to make money — real money, that is.' There was a steel stubbornness under his soft tone that told her it was useless to argue.

'All right,' Diana said and gave a defeated sigh, 'we'll do it your way.'

Matt studied her for a moment. She reminded him of a hurt little girl. He sat up and gently caressed her shoulder.

'We don't have to settle everything tonight, do we?' She shook her head. He drew her to him and their lips met softly.

* * *

It was a little before ten o'clock when Cole Devlin, Jesse Hayne and Shank, who was leading a saddled horse, turned into a dark alley that ran behind the Cut and Shoot Saloon. They walked their mounts slowly, scanning the shadows for sleeping vagrants, passed-out drunks, and amorous couples with no place better to go. None were about. From all the ruckus inside the saloon, nobody should be interested in them. As they pulled up behind the saloon, Emmet Wade stepped out of the shadows and moved to Cole.

'Sutton's girl ain't been down yet,' he said in a low, worried tone. 'Maybe she's gonna stay up in her room with him all night.'

'Then we'll just have to go fetch her,' Cole said easily. Saddle leather creaked as the three men dismounted. Cole stood before Emmet. 'You go on back inside and tell your Jenny to talk with the guard on the stairs.' Emmet nodded and turned to leave. Cole caught his arm. 'Then you come back here and watch the horses, while we go up the back stairs.'

'Not them stairs,' Emmet said nervously. 'They lead to Jack Rath's private rooms.'

Devlin shrugged. 'Then we'll use the side stairs.'

'The door at the top is locked.'

'You ever heard of a door that can't be opened?'

Emmet looked sheepish, and left without answering.

Devlin and the men moved about stretching their tired muscles and thinking about what was to come. He had been dirt poor nearly all of his thirty-five years, just like his old man, an Arkansas farmer. Sure, he'd made some money during his outlaw career, but he'd spent it just as fast on enjoying the good things of life. Well, tonight he was 'inheriting' a windfall of money, and, by damn, things were gonna be different!

* * *

In his denims and boots, Matt Sutton stood shaving in front of a gilt-framed oval mirror on the wall. He'd just finished the right side of his face when he saw Diana's reflection as she stepped from behind her dressing screen. The sight made him quickly lower the razor, for fear of cutting his throat. Putting down the razor, he turned and ran his eyes over her costume — or what there was of it.

The black, one-piece theatrical costume with a corseted waist revealed plenty of cleavage and legs and displayed her statuesque magnificence to its advantage. Black fish-net tights and slender high-heeled shoes completed the outfit. Her ivory skin and honey-blonde hair that cascaded almost to the middle of her back were a startling and intriguing contrast.

For a long instant Matt just stood staring while she posed seductively beside the screen. Then he cleared his throat and said, 'You oughta know better than to dress like that in front of a man fresh-new from prison.'

She beamed, pleased by his reaction, and walked to him. 'These are my working clothes.'

'Who can concentrate on cards with you looking that way?' She batted her long-lashed eyes innocently. His eyes roamed to the rumpled bed, then back to her.

Diana quickly backed away shaking her head at him emphatically. 'No you don't, Matt', she said lightly. 'I have to go downstairs and work for an hour or so,' — gracefully she evaded his grasping hands — 'and I can't get all mussed up.'

Grinning playfully, Matt moved after

her as she backed toward the sitting-room. 'Rath's customers can do without you for one whole night.'

'Now, Matt . . . ' Diana warned, laughing. He caught her in the doorway and kissed her. Her muffled protests had just become passionate moans when there was a knock at the door. They broke off reluctantly, with Matt still keeping a tight hold on her, and Diana glanced over her shoulder and called, 'Who is it?'

'Message from Mr Rath, Miss Logan,' answered an indistinct voice.

'Just a minute,' Diana said, then gently but firmly pushed Matt back into the bedroom with both hands against his chest. 'You get in there and finish shaving before you get me into trouble,' she said in mock sternness. She pulled the door shut, then turned, drew a composing breath, and hurried across the room. She unlocked the hall door and opened it to find herself staring into the face of an ugly, bearded giant.

In spite of his size, Shank moved very fast. His right arm encircled Diana's waist before she could recover from her surprise and locked her against him, while his left hand clamped over her mouth as he moved into the room with her. Jesse rushed in after him, taking a bunch of white clothes' line from under his frayed, wool-collared jacket, and Cole entered last, closing and locking the door behind them.

Recovering from her surprise, Diana kicked Shank in the shin, then stamped on his instep and ground with her high heel; a trick she'd learned to discourage the unwanted attention of amorous saloon drunks. The big man let out a pained gasp and loosened his hold. Diana sank her teeth into his fleshy hand and, with a scream, twisted free of his clutching hands. She shouted Matt's name and started for the bedroom. Snarling, Shank lunged, seized a handful of her flying hair and yanked her back to him.

Razor in hand, Matt appeared in the

bedroom doorway and stared out at Diana and the men. A red mist swam before his eyes, anger so searing that it robbed him of all coherent thought, and he charged straight at Shank. Jesse lunged to intercept him. Without breaking his stride Matt slammed a fist into Jesse's face and sent him sprawling out of his way.

Seeing Matt bearing down on him with the razor, Shank backhanded Diana to the floor, where she lay, stunned, and moved forward. He caught Matt's wrist in a crushing grip and twisted the razor from his hand.

It fell to the floor and was then sent skidding under the sofa by the men's feet.

Matt smashed Shank in the face with his other hand, then jerked his wrist free and whaled into him with both fists. The giant rocked on his heels, glowered and lashed out at Matt.

But Matt wasn't there.

Matt ducked, knocked Shank off-balance with his shoulder, and caught him on the jaw with an over-handed blow. Then he stepped in and pounded Shank's belly, feeling his fists sink in solidly. A huge fist clubbed the side of his head. Matt rolled with the blow and came back swinging.

He was so lost in his rage that he failed to see or hear Cole Devlin move up behind him with his Colt drawn. As Matt bobbed back to avoid Shank's head butt, Devlin swung his six-gun. The long barrel connected sharply with the back of Matt's head.

A blinding light exploded in Matt's brain. Then blackness took its place. And he fell forward, headlong into a pitch-dark pit.

4

Jack Rath was relaxing in the sitting-room of his apartment, reading a book while listening to the phonograph he'd had sent all the way from New York City. It was his pride and joy, not to mention status symbol. No one else in town, perhaps not even the whole territory, owned one. It was just winding down when he heard sounds of a struggle in Diana Logan's adjoining apartment.

That was strange. Somehow he didn't think they'd begin arguing so soon after being reunited. But then people did change over the years, especially someone who'd been in prison. He hoped the argument wasn't too serious; it was simpler to keep track of Sutton if he had the girl with him.

Draining his whiskey glass, Rath rose and walked to the wall separating the two apartments. He placed the rim of the glass against the wall and put an ear to its bottom. The muffled voices became distinct, and he was both surprised and relieved to learn that the two had unexpected visitors — and very unwelcome ones at that. He debated sending his men to help, then decided to wait. This incident might just make Sutton try for the money faster than he'd intended. He kept his ear to the glass and continued listening intently.

* * *

Matt painfully rolled his head in the direction of the sofa, groggily saw Diana's trim, black-stockinged ankles, and stared in confusion at the contrasting loop of white clothes' line about them. Then his mind cleared and, bristling with rage, he tried to sit up. He grimaced at the shooting pain at the back of his head and the ropes cutting into his wrists and booted ankles. His vision momentarily blurred, then cleared and he saw Cole Devlin's grinning face.

'Devlin . . . what the hell . . . ' he began, his words slurred.

'Whoa, now,' Cole said in good humour, 'don't go gittin' riled, or I'm liable to think you ain't pleasured to see me.'

Fighting off the wrenching pain dancing up and down his neck and spine, Matt shoved himself up onto an elbow. 'You're wasting your time,' he said, his voice dead flat. 'There's no money.'

Cole shook his head and said in mock reproach, 'Matt, I am ashamed for you. Why we ain't no more than howdied, and right off you commence to tellin' lies.'

'Lemme kick him a couple o' three times, Cole,' Shank growled, drawing back a huge boot.

'Hear that, Matt?' Cole said, eyeing him with a wounded expression. 'You're upsettin' the boys,' — he stroked

Diana's bare shoulder — 'and makin' yourself even smaller in the eyes of your woman.' Diana eyed him coldly above her bandanna gag.

'Get your damn hands off her, Devlin!' Matt ordered.

'Or you'll what?' Colt asked in mock amazement. 'Crawl over here and bite me on the ankle, like one of them ladies' lap dogs?' While Matt fumed impotently, Cole turned Diana's face to his and caressed her long hair with his free hand. 'I always tried to sit close to Matt on visitin' times,' he confided, 'just so's I could look at you.' She tried to turn away, but he held her chin. 'I did a lot of thinkin' about you on them long, lonely nights.' He grinned and nodded. 'Yes sir, I surely did.'

'Devlin, I told you in prison,' Matt said firmly, 'and now I'm telling you again — I don't know where that money is.'

Cole ran a hand along Diana's cheek, tracing the outline of her face. 'Powerful nice woman you got here, Matt . . . '

Matt's eyes narrowed on him. 'Sure be a shame if somethin' bad was to happen to her on account of your stinginess.'

'She's got nothing to do with this!'

Devlin smiled and chucked Diana under her chin. 'And I say she does.' His barely parted lips didn't move with his quiet words. Diana's cool look vanished into nervousness. His smile unchanged, Cole grabbed a handful of her hair and took a vicious twist. Diana emitted a sharp muffled cry as her head was roughly forced over the back of the couch.

'Let her alone!' Matt shouted, yanking at his ropes, oblivious to the hurt.

'Not till you remember about the money,' Cole said, his voice going softer, eyes on Diana's pained face. His free hand crudely caressed her shoulder. In a sudden blur of motion, he slapped and back-handed her face, then slammed a fist into her taut midriff. Face contorting in frenzied torment, Diana gasped into her gag and, delicate nostrils flaring for air, spasmed wildly.

'Stop it!' Matt yelled, thrashing madly. 'I'll tell you!'

Cole released Diana and sat forward on the edge of the sofa, grinning down at Matt. 'I knowed you could be reasonable.' Diana hunched forward, trying to draw her knees up to her pain-quivering body, and sobbed softly into her gag. Cole placed a hand on her bare back and stroked her gently. 'Otherwise, she might just hurt herself again.'

'I'm gonna kill you for that, Devlin,' Matt promised solemnly, flames of hatred banking behind his eyes.

'You're welcome to try,' Cole said pleasantly, '*after* I git that money.'

'I don't have it on me. And I can't get to it right away because I'm being watched by a Pinkerton man.'

'You'll find a way — if you ever hope to see her alive again.' His eyes locked on Matt's for a long moment, letting the threat sink in. Matt nodded, silently cursing his helplessness. Cole glanced to Jesse. 'Fetch her somethin' to wear over what she's got on. We don't want her catchin' pneumonia ridin' around in the cold night air, do we?' Jesse turned and strode into the bedroom.

'I'll take you to the money — but she stays here.'

Devlin smiled knowingly. 'What — and have you lead me all over the desert like a blind man while you're waitin' for the chance to kill me?' He laughed throatily, and drew Diana upright by her hair. 'We'll do it my way. You bring me the money, and I give you her.' His lips peeled back in a wide, pleased grin. 'That's a fair enough trade, ain't it?'

Matt kept silent. Devlin was set on having his way. Black despair set in as he saw Jesse come out of the bedroom carrying a hooded riding cape.

'That'll do fine,' Cole said, standing and taking the cape. 'Now untie her ankles and we'll be on our way.' While Jesse busied himself, Cole looked down at Matt. 'Meet us at the stock pens on the edge of town tomorrow night at ten, and we'll put an end to our business.'

Matt considered, then shook his head. 'I got a long ride ahead of me — that's cutting it too fine.' He felt a heart-twisting jerk as he saw Diana tense, disappointment plain on her face. It couldn't be helped; he needed every minute he could get.

Cole scowled, swung his gaze to Diana as Jesse drew her to her wobbly feet, then back to Matt. 'Midnight, then.'

'Done,' Matt agreed. That was still cutting it pretty fine, but he hated the thought of Diana spending any more time than was necessary with Devlin.

'Oughtn't to take you too long to slip them ropes, but it'll be enough for us to git a good head start.' Cole draped the cape around Diana's shoulders, hiding her tied wrists, and pulled the hood up over her head. 'Don't waste no time tryin' to trail us,' he said, his voice suddenly ugly and threatening,' 'cause I'll kill her right off. And that'll also happen if you go to hollerin' soon as we git out the door.' He drew Diana to Matt's side. 'Take a long look at her,' he said, his voice taking on a sarcastic tone, 'just so's you don't disremember what you'll be losin' if you don't show up tomorrow night.'

Matt's nerves tingled as he solemnly read Devlin's threat and saw Diana's pale, nervous face staring out at him from inside the cape's black hood. His own helplessness suddenly made him feel brittle and used up. He couldn't let on to her. 'I'll be there, Diana,' he said, summoning confidence into his face and voice with a fierce wrenching of inner will. 'I promise you nothing is gonna keep me away.' He was rewarded by the love and trust that shone in her large blue eyes. She gasped and tried to go to her knees beside him. Devlin quickly restrained her.

'We done jawed long enough,' he said, turning Diana away and herding her toward the door. The other two men followed. 'Don't be late neither, Matt,' Devlin said, almost as an afterthought, without turning around.

A cold hand closed over Matt's heart as he watched them go, and heard their hurried footsteps fade from the door. He then threw himself against his ropes.

* * *

Jack Rath took the glass from the wall and smiled thoughtfully. That little bit of eavesdropping was going to bring him $50,000. Thanks to Cole Devlin it would be his for the taking tomorrow night. He walked to a decanter beside the phonograph and poured himself a liberal drink.

After offering a silent toast to his unexpected good fortune, Rath cranked the phonograph, picked up his book, and settled into his easy chair. He found that his mind was too preoccupied to concentrate on reading, so he contented himself with listening to the lilting Strauss waltz and laying plans for tomorrow night.

5

Emmet Wade stood nervously waiting with the horses as Diana and the men came up. He flushed and turned his eyes as she recognized him and her surprise quickly became scorn. She realized that Jenny Taylor must also be involved. Being an outlaw's girl, Diana had few friends in Bedlow and she had considered Jenny to be one of her closest. She was hurt and saddened that Jenny would repay her past kindness like this. Then she solemnly thought that with $50,000 at stake friendships are quickly forgotten.

Diana was jarred from her gloomy thoughts as Shank swept her up as though she were a feather and placed her in a saddle. Then he and Jesse tied her ankles to the stirrups.

Cole swung up into his saddle and looked down at Emmet. 'Go on back inside and tell Jenny to keep her eyes and ears open, and to let us know if there's any trouble about her disappearin'.' Emmet nodded, still unable to meet Diana's eyes. 'Then git your horse and catch up to us.' Emmet muttered and, eager to escape Diana's accusing eyes, hurried into the shadows. Cole flashed Diana a broad grin, took her reins, and they started off. Jesse and Shank followed.

Diana threw a helpless glance back at the saloon and desperately hoped Matt would appear, guns blazing.

He didn't.

★ ★ ★

Wrists bruised and torn, Matt Sutton lay exhausted on the carpet. Luckily his boots protected his ankles from the taut ropes, but that didn't keep them from aching something fierce. Desperately he knew he had to free his hands soon, before his fingers became too numb and swollen to be useful.

Sure Devlin's bunch had left town by now, but it wouldn't do to raise a ruckus. Being found like this would only invite unwanted questions. And with Diana gone, it wouldn't take much thought for Rath or Gillum to put things together. He must get free by himself and then get to that money fast, without any interference.

Suddenly something under the sofa caught his eye. He'd been so deep in thought that he'd been staring at it not realizing what he saw.

It was his razor.

Now the problem was to get to it.

Gathering his remaining strength, Matt rolled to the sofa. It was only three or four steps away but the effort was tiring. He lay gasping for a short while, then, pushing with his hands and straining his stomach muscles, laboriously he forced his body up to a sitting position and manoeuvred himself around with his back against the sofa. He drew his legs up, dug his heels into the carpet and shoved. Slowly the sofa inched backwards. It took a couple more shoves before the razor was finally uncovered. Then he began the tedious, exhausting work of awkwardly severing his ropes without slicing open his wrists.

Finally he was free, impatiently snapping the partly sawed rope with his own strength. He brought his hands in front and, disregarding the agonizing tinglings, sawed through the knot that bound his ankles. He dragged himself up and staggered into the bedroom, where he hastily tended his rope-torn wrists and finished dressing.

★ ★ ★

Jack Rath was drinking alone at his private table when Rio urgently shoved his way through the crowded saloon and strode up to him.

'Spence just seen Sutton heading for the livery stable,' the gunman informed him, a trace of emotion in his usually toneless voice. 'You want us to follow him?'

'There's no need,' Rath replied.

A flicker of emotion played over Rio's usually stoic features. 'But what if he's going after the money?'

'Don't concern yourself,' Rath said casually, enjoying the game. 'Things are working out even better than I had hoped.' He was amused by Rio's bewilderment, then decided to share his knowledge. Nothing impressed and kept underlings in line more than their employer knowing all about a situation before they did. But before he could do so, Norton stomped up to the table.

'Mr Rath, some of the customers been asking for Diana,' the bearded man announced.

'Tell them she won't be dealing faro tonight or tomorrow night.'

Norton nodded, puzzled, and lumbered away. Rath saw that Rio was just as puzzled. Diana had become a regular attraction at the Cut and Shoot. Men came and willingly lost their money just for the privilege of gawking at the tall blonde beauty's magnificent, briefly attired figure and exchanging a few hopeful words with her. They were always rebuffed and forced to seek their pleasures in the arms of one of the more amenable girls. But the fools kept coming back on the slim chance that one night she might change her mind.

Rath turned his attention back to Rio. 'Relax and join me in a drink,' he said, indicating a chair. Pleased, the gunman sat, his eyes on the expensive bottle of whiskey before them. Rath smiled and poured another glass.

It was also wise to occasionally display generosity, however small, to the hired help.

* * *

Matt Sutton reached Turner's Livery Stable by a roundabout way and was pretty sure he hadn't been followed. He was relieved to see that the stableman wasn't about. He wanted to slip out of town before anyone was aware he was gone, even though that meant leaving his guns at the jailhouse. He'd just have to trust that he wouldn't need them on the trail. But there was something he did need, and he saw it amongst a stack of tools leaning against an empty stall.

Matt discarded the long handle shovel in favour of a short spade and then saddled his sorrel. He wrapped the spade in his coat and tied it behind his saddle. There was no sense advertising that he was going digging. He led the horse to the wide double doors, pushed one open some and looked out.

The area around the stable was deserted. Further down the main street there was some coming and going from the saloons.

Matt led the horse out, shoved the door closed, then mounted and rode off at a rapid trot.

★ ★ ★

73

A match flared in the mouth of a dark alley catty-cornered to the livery stable and briefly illuminated Lew Gillum's smiling face as he lit his thin cigar. He lingered there savouring the smoke until Matt Sutton was out of town. Then he stepped from the alley and strolled to a nearby hitching rail where his pinto stood, three-legged, with several others. He mounted and rode off unhurriedly, determined to keep a comfortable distance between him and Sutton.

★ ★ ★

The group reined in before the cabin and the men dismounted. Devlin gave orders, then stood beaming like a child watching his Christmas present being unwrapped while Shank and Jesse untied Diana's ankles from the stirrups. Angrily she tried to flinch away from his reaching hand, but he caught her arm and pulled her from the saddle.

'Settle down, honey,' Cole said good-naturedly. 'I ain't gonna do nothin' but untie you.' She arched a sceptical eyebrow but stopped her struggles. He tossed her cape back and fumbled with her ropes, then pulled down her hood and untied her gag. 'There, now ain't that better?' Diana was coldly silent. He took her arm and pulled her toward the cabin.

As they entered, Diane was immediately assaulted by a variety of smells, few of them pleasant. Dust, age, stale tobacco smoke, and body odour stubbornly refused to be displaced by the aroma of coffee and boiled venison stew on the potbellied stove. Three bunks and a table and chairs were the room's only furnishings.

'This place ain't fancy,' Cole said, waving an arm about, 'but you just make do and don't give us no trouble . . . ' — he flashed a reassuring grin — 'and you'll be back with ole Matt 'fore you know it.' Diana found no comfort in his words.

The door opened and Rose stepped out. She wore a short black leather vest laced together with rawhide thongs, which showed a more than modest view of her bosom, matching snug leather pants and knee-length, high-heeled boots. A thin leather belt with a sheathed hunting knife attached emphasized her trim waist. Parted in the middle, her raven's wing hair cascaded down far below her shoulders. She stood posed in the doorway for effect and favoured Devlin with a sultry smile. 'I'm glad you're back safe, Cole.'

He grinned and took in what he was supposed to. 'Well, looky at you . . . I ain't seen you wearin' that in a month of Sundays.'

Rose moved toward him, graceful, catlike. 'Tonight's special, ain't it, honey?' She took his arm and snuggled against him, making it very clear to Diana that he was hers.

'Yeah, it ain't every night we got company,' Cole said pleasantly, and turned Diana toward Rose. The movement made Diana's cape part, revealing her skimpy costume beneath.

Rose gaped at the costume and Diana's splendid figure, then angrily found her voice. 'Why's she wearin' that?'

'She works in a saloon,' Cole said simply.

'Well, I don't like it!'

'What the hell's got into you?' Cole asked, exasperated.

Before Rose could reply, the front door opened and Jesse and Shank stomped in. 'Emmet's on lookout, and the horses are put away,' Jesse announced. The two men stopped and, sensing the tension, looked back and forth between Rose and Diana. Cole quickly took advantage of the distraction and headed for the back room with Diana.

'Good enough. I'll take first watch with her. Rose, you fix supper.'

Rose went after them, grabbed Diana's other arm and wrenched her from his grasp. '*I'll* watch her!' Cole stared in surprise as Rose roughly dragged the blonde girl toward the back room. 'But what about supper?' he asked innocently.

Rose shoved Diana inside the room and glanced back at him. 'It's on the stove. You can heat it up!' She disappeared into the room, slammed the door and then bolted it.

Frowning, Cole shook his head and looked to Jesse and Shank. 'I swear she's gittin' squirrelier by the day.' The men remained silent. Content that he still had until late tomorrow night to take that good-lookin' blonde, whether Rose liked it or not, Cole ambled to the stove and began heating the stew and coffee.

6

Once away from Bedlow, Matt Sutton drove the sorrel hard. He wanted to cover as much of the long ride as he could at night while it was cool. When the sun came up the desert would be hot as hell, and he couldn't risk losing his horse by maintaining a dead run. Still, he couldn't pamper it either. He had to reach where he was going and return before midnight tomorrow. Diana's life depended on it.

Jawline tight, Matt grimly wondered if the money would save either of them. He didn't trust Cole Devlin as far as he could spit. He'd shared a prison cell with Devlin for well over a year and knew that he was a cunning, ice-cold killer. And they both knew that after the trade was over he would hunt Devlin down and kill him, no matter where he hid.

Matt pushed aside those thoughts. If his figuring was right, he'd be back in Bedlow with just enough time to spare to lay some plans of his own.

* * *

Several miles behind, Lew Gillum leisurely followed Matt Sutton's trail, cautiously keeping to the shadowy, rocky twisting foothills whenever possible. The full moon was a mixed blessing. It made the hoof prints easy enough to track, but it would reveal him to Sutton if he got too close. He idly wondered what the all-fired hurry was; Sutton wasn't even taking care to try to cover his trail.

For twenty years Gillum had tracked men, and with each one he learned something about his character, how he thought and so on. He knew Sutton for a cautious man, and this behaviour just didn't fit him. Something was goading him besides greed. But, what the hell — the sooner Sutton got the money, the sooner he could take it away from him.

* * *

Clutching her cape about her, Diana sat stiffly on the edge of the bunk in the back room of the cabin and stared at the strange, unsettling shadows cast by a lamp on a nearby stool. Rose sat stoically in a chair placed to one side of the door, her dark, brooding eyes upon her. Diana could feel the half-breed girl's jealousy and hate clear across the room. An exceptional beauty, she was used to the jealousies of other women, but before now none had ever really wanted to harm her. And, despite working in a saloon, this was the first time she'd ever found herself in a dangerous situation.

She had been born in a tiny East Texas town near the Louisiana border. Her father had been a doctor, but that had not kept her mother from dying in childbirth. Then, when she was five years old, a yellow fever epidemic hit the town, and her father had sent her away from the bayou country to live with her only other relative, her Aunt Harriet, while he stayed to nurse the sick. His noble act had been in vain. He died, and the few survivors had burned the town and left.

Aunt Harriet was ten years older than her father, and had been a great beauty in her day. Her late husband had been a riverboat gambler, and had won the farm, which was a few miles outside of Austin, in a poker game. It had been Aunt Harriet who'd taught her how to handle a deck of cards. It had been merely for amusement, until Harriet's death.

The South was still being bled by the carpetbaggers and their local toadies, and the seizure of the farm (less than a year before the Reconstruction had ended) had left Diana homeless, but with more than a few Yankee proposals — some even of marriage. She'd told them all what they could do with their proposals. Then she'd left Texas with only a suitcase and a deck of cards and had never looked back. That had been over four years ago.

A knock at the door, followed by Cole Devlin's voice, snapped Diana out of her reverie. She stiffened, her eyes darting to the door as Rose stood and answered him.

'C'mon out, Rose-honey,' Devlin replied casually, 'we're gonna eat.'

Rose opened the door. Devlin stood in the doorway, grinning 'What about her?' she asked, jerking a thumb toward Diana.

'Jesse's bringin' her plate,' Cole answered, putting on his best innocent expression as her face darkened with suspicion. He stepped back from the doorway and beckoned her out. 'Well, come ahead on, honey.'

Relaxing, Rose smiled and stepped outside, only to have Cole slither through the doorway sideways before she realized what he was up to. 'Cole, what are you doin'?' she cried, as he slammed and bolted the door from the inside. The only reply was Cole's gloating chuckle. She pounded and kicked at the door in a wild rage.

Cole turned from the door and grinned over at Diana, who quickly rose from the bunk and eyed him warily. 'Now don't go gittin' spooked,' he said over Rose's commotion outside. 'I just want ta talk.' He took a step forward and Diana stiffly edged away from the bunk, clutching her cape to her. He stopped. She continued her retreat.

* * *

Unconcerned, Jesse and Shank sat at the table shovelling in their stew as Rose screamed in frustration and gave the door a final kick, then spun and stormed from the cabin. After a moment or two of thought, Jesse slowly pushed back his plate and stood.

'Aw, why don't you sit down and

finish your supper?' Shank suggested, as he chewed a cheek-bulging mouthful. Jesse paid him no mind and silently went out after Rose. The big man shrugged in dismissal and proceeded to scrape Jesse's leavings onto his own plate.

Jesse saw Rose hunched over near one side of the cabin, struggling with a heavy rock she was toting. She started around the corner, but he caught her arm. 'What're you aimin' to do with that boulder?' he asked dryly.

'I'm gonna bust out the back window an — ' She broke off with a squeal as the rock slipped from her hands, nearly crushing her booted toes. She jerked her arm free and, panting from exhaustion, whirled on Jesse. 'Now look what you made me do!'

'Why don't you settle down and quit makin' a fool of yourself?' he asked calmly.

'*I'm* his woman, Jesse!' she cried, almost plaintively.

'And that's why you oughtn't to be

85

takin' on so.' She frowned and began to regain her composure. Now that he held her attention, Jesse continued. 'That woman ain't nothin' up alongside of you — just a buncha paint and frills. Why you got her beat six ways to sundown.' Rose softened at the compliments. Then he added, almost as an afterthought, 'And Cole knows it.'

'Then what's he doin' in there with her?'

'Aw, that's just business,' Jesse lied reassuringly. Rose leaned against the side of the window and pondered his words.

★ ★ ★

Cole Devlin grinned, anticipating his conquest, as the blonde abruptly realized that she'd backed herself into a corner. His grin slipped a hair when she quickly pulled off a shoe and menacingly brandished its high heel as a weapon. She glared hatred at him, the soft strength in her exquisite face warned that she meant business. He stood with his hands on his hips and looked suitably intimidated.

'Yes sir,' Cole said in a soft, pleasant drawl, 'I surely admire a high-spirited woman . . . ' He made his move swiftly, like a cat pouncing, and caught her wrist as she swung. With a savage twist he forced the shoe from her hand and then pinned her to the wall with his body. 'Makes a man know she's worth havin',' he said, finishing his words. She gasped and tried to get at his eyes with her long red nails, intent on clawing them out. He forced her hands to either side of her head, held them there and kissed her viciously.

Diana wildly rolled her head from side to side and managed to break his kiss, only to have his insistent mouth force itself back onto her lips. She sank her teeth into his lower lip and was sickened by the salty taste of blood. As his head reared back in surprise, she tore a hand free and raked the side of his face with her nails. He staggered back a step, his hand going to his cheek, and she rammed her knee up into his groin.

Cole yelped as a sickening agony shot up through his middle and staggered back on jellied legs. Diana tried to break past, but was slowed by only one shoe. His weakly pawing hand grabbed her shoulder. She frantically twisted free, leaving him holding her cape. But before she could take a step, Cole let loose with a haymaker that connected solidly under her chin and lifted her right off the floor. Her head snapped back, smacked the wall hard. With a soft moan, Diana went limp and wilted down the wall to the floor.

For a time Cole stood over her, looking with hungry eyes at the unconscious, scantily clad beauty. Then he groaned and asked aloud, 'Why'd I have to go and do that for?'

★ ★ ★

Arms folded across her breasts, Rose leaned against the cabin and listened, enthralled, to all the pretty words that Jesse was attributing to Cole. Like every woman she longed to hear words of endearment and reassurance that her love was returned in kind. 'Does Cole *really* say all them nice things about me?' she asked coyly, anxious to hear more.

Jesse placed a splay-fingered hand beside her head and braced himself, stiff-armed, against the wall. 'He sure enough does.' This was the first time he'd been able to say the things he felt to her, and crediting them to Cole made the words come easy. Now that Devlin fancied Sutton's woman maybe Rose would turn to him. She was only twenty and he was old enough to be her pa and then some, but, damn it all, he truly loved her and would do right by her. He slowly bent his elbow, letting his body lean in toward her.

'Jesse, I . . . ' Rose began, uncomfortable as his face neared hers.

A door slammed loudly inside the cabin. Jesse quickly recoiled from Rose as they both flinched, startled. She anxiously peered through the window, saw Cole and hurried to the cabin door. Silently cussing his lost chance, Jesse followed bleakly.

As Rose reached the door, Cole stepped out. The bright moonlight revealed the scratches on his cheek. 'What did she do,' Rose asked, feigning innocence, 'try to scalp you?'

Cole scowled, touched his cheek and looked past her at Jesse. 'I'm spellin' Emmet. You take over in a couple of hours.' He stalked off without waiting for a reply, leaving Rose hurt and sullen.

Rose rushed into the cabin and, seeing her Injun-mad look, Jesse hurried in behind her. She tore across the cabin, threw open the door and stalked inside.

The sight that greeted Rose cooled her anger and brought a satisfied smile. The golden-haired girl with skin as pale as a fish's belly lay sprawled unconscious in a corner.

Rose stood staring, biting her lower lip, her eyes glittering with hate, then she became aware of Jesse entering the room. She drew a deep breath and turned to him. 'You go on, Jesse. I'll watch her from here on.' He hesitated, uncertain. She smiled. 'She ain't gonna be no trouble tonight.' Jesse went out and Rose closed and bolted the door. Then she went to the bunk and made herself comfortable.

After all, the white squaw sure wouldn't be needing it tonight. She knew from painful experience that when Cole thumped you one, you stayed down — for a very long time.

★ ★ ★

The grey-black sky was giving way to a rosy tint as the red ball of sun slowly made its appearance above the rim of the horizon. Sunrise, beautiful or otherwise, was the last thing Matt Sutton wanted to see. Soon the desert was going to be oven-hot, impeding the progress of man and beast, and sucking the life juices from their bodies. Luckily he'd covered most of the distance that night. But there was still the ride back, a lot of which must be made during the day.

The sorrel was beginning to stumble with fatigue. Matt sympathized; he was tired to the core himself. He slowed the animal to a fast trot. There would be time for a couple of bursts of speed before the sun was high enough for its baking heat to be felt. After that, travel would be slow.

Matt turned in the saddle and looked back at the bleak foothills. There was no sign of life. Still, he had an itchy feeling that he wasn't alone out here. He turned back and eased the sorrel into a gallop.

★ ★ ★

Back in the foothills, Lew Gillum trudged along leading his tired pinto.

Unlike Sutton, he was in no great hurry and was conserving his horse's strength. He took his canteen from the saddle, unscrewed the top and drank sparingly. Then he gave a couple of handfuls of water to the horse before returning the canteen to the saddle.

Gillum stood watching the lone column of dust rising off at the horizon from Sutton's horse. It appeared he was intent on racing the rising sun, trying to gain a few more miles before it was up good. Gillum sighed heavily, fully aware of what the sun's rays were going to bring, and climbed back into the saddle.

Then doggedly he continued his pursuit.

7

It was early morning as Jenny Taylor uncertainly approached the mountain cabin. She was eager to learn if Emmet was safe, and her guilty conscience also preyed on her about Diana Logan's safety. She drew a deep, composing breath and gently pulled up her mount in front of the cabin. The door instantly flew open and Emmet happily barged out to greet her and help her dismount. She was tired from her long ride and clung to him for support.

'Emmet, I was worried sick about you,' Jenny said and embraced him.

'Everythin' went just fine, Jenny,' Emmet said, holding her and not wanting to let go, even though he knew Cole and Jesse were probably watching from inside.

Jenny drew back and looked him in

the eye. 'Is Diana all right?' she asked tensely.

'Yeah, Rose is watchin' over her like a mother hen.' He smiled, amused, and added, 'She won't let Cole or nobody in the room with them.' Jenny gave an audible sigh of relief. He took her arm. 'You want ta go in and see for yourself?'

Jenny gasped and sharply pulled away. 'Oh, no . . . I couldn't face her!'

Emmet was startled by the intensity of her reaction, then remembered his own earlier guilt feelings. 'I'm sorry, Jenny, I only thought . . . '

She took his arm and looked up at him with large imploring brown eyes. 'Please . . . couldn't we stay out here?'

'Sure,' Emmet said, slipping an arm around her slim waist and leading her out of earshot of the cabin.

★ ★ ★

Cole Devlin stood peering out the cabin window at Emmet and the tall blonde girl in riding clothes. From a distance she sure reminded him of the blonde woman in the back room. He didn't blame Emmet for raving about his girl at the saloon. So many of them girls had faces that would stop a clock, and since Emmet weren't no real prize hisself he sorta figured his girl would be the same. This came as a sure enough surprise.

'Once Sutton's got his woman back,' Jesse asked, from the table, where he sat expertly making himself a cigarette, 'what's to stop him from shootin' right then and there?'

Cole smiled; sometimes ole Jesse wasn't as dumb as he looked. The same thought had been nagging him since last night. 'Maybe we'll keep her a spell longer,' he said, his eyes fixed on Jenny Taylor.

Jesse finished flaking the tobacco onto the paper, licked it and rolled it neatly. He stuck the cigarette in his mouth and talked around it. 'How we gonna do that when she's part of the trade?' He took a match from a shirt pocket, scratched it on the table and brought the flame up to the end of his cigarette.

'I'm schemin' on that right now,' Cole said thoughtfully, his eyes still on Jenny.

★ ★ ★

Matt Sutton suddenly reined in his horse and leaned down, squinting at the desert floor. The trail was there plain enough. A party of unshod horses, eight of them, had crossed slowly in single file. The prints weren't more than twelve hours old, if that. A discarded headband told him they were Apaches. Probably up from Mexico on a raid.

Matt's eyes followed the tracks until they disappeared into the scrub. As long as they kept right on going in that direction there was no danger of a meeting. This explained the feeling he had about not being alone out here. And him without a weapon to his name. He was a damned fool to have left Bedlow so unprepared. But who could have expected rampaging Apaches?

* * *

The sun was high in the sky when Matt Sutton crested a boulder-strewn hill and stared down at the one-street ghost town, less than a dozen sagging buildings ranging along either side of its length. He'd lost time getting here, covering the remaining five miles from where he'd seen the Apache signs very slowly, as warily as a wolf. Better to be safe than dead. If he tended to things quickly there should still be time to return to Bedlow well ahead of midnight.

Matt studied the town. It appeared safe, but he wasn't a trusting man — not with Apaches in the area. He reflected with irony that the last time he'd been here he was in a big hurry too — just one jump ahead of a posse. He and Jake Caskie had buried the money in boot hill, then high-tailed it away. The posse had caught up with them the next day, and that was when Jake had bought it.

Matt roused himself from his memories and guided the sorrel down toward the town, where $50,000 was waiting to be claimed.

★ ★ ★

Back a'ways, Lew Gillum sat his pinto in a draw and watched Sutton's tall, rangy figure disappear over the crest of the hill. He knew that the old ghost town of Crystal Flats was Sutton's destination; otherwise, he wouldn't have made such slow progress after leaving those Indian signs.

Gillum dismounted and stretched his legs. He'd give Sutton time to ride the short distance to town before starting across the open expanse. He grinned and tried to imagine Sutton's reaction when he arrived and took the money from him.

* * *

Matt Sutton rode slowly down the middle of the street, his sharp eyes warily scanning the decaying, skeletal line of flat buildings, bleached by the elements. The light wind sent dust and tumbleweeds swirling along the street and made sagging doors and shutters slam and creak on their hinges. He rode through town and out to the cemetery, about twenty-five yards past the last building.

Matt dismounted before what was left of the wooden fence and found that his legs were shaky from his long ride. His head was swimming from lack of sleep. He untied the bundle behind his saddle, removed the spade from his coat and headed into the graveyard.

As Matt stumbled about searching, his concern mounted on finding that

100

many of the wooden grave markers had either fallen or been scattered. It took a bit of patience, but he located a fallen marker with the words: 'Jeb Parker, Hossthief'. Then he sank the spade into the earth and began to dig.

When he was a little past two feet down, Matt began to widen the hole rather than deepen it. His heart was pounding excitedly. Then the spade dug into something that gave a little under the pressure of its pointed head. Matt's breath caught in his chest. His mouth went dry. His thudding heartbeat seemed loud in the funereal silence. He continued digging, slowly and carefully, clearing away the earth that covered a burlap sack wrapped around a bulky object. Discarding the spade, he dropped down and began hastily clawing away the last bit of dirt with both hands. Then he lifted the heavy sack from the hole.

A quick look put his mind at ease that no prairie dog or other burrowing varmint had gotten to the sack and its contents. Hands shaking from excitement and fatigue, Matt tore open the burlap and removed the bulging saddle-bags. The leather was still in good condition. He tugged open one of the flaps and dug into the pocket. His hand came out with a stack of bills. They were intact, so were the other neat stacks, still in their bank wrappers. He was so concentrated on the precious contents that Gillum's voice took him completely by surprise.

'They sure look pretty, don't they, Sutton?'

Dropping the bills back into the mouth of the leather pocket, Matt whirled and saw the Pinkerton man a few yards away, six-gun trained on him. Dammit, this was the last thing he'd expected. Gillum cautiously edged forward.

'I didn't expect you to move this soon.' He grinned unpleasantly. 'Guess our talk did some good after all.'

'Don't flatter yourself, Gillum.'

Gillum stopped near him and

motioned with his free hand. 'Throw 'em here, nice and easy.' The bags landed heavily, stirring dust around Gillum's feet. 'All right, stand up.'

Matt climbed to his feet. 'Gillum, you gotta help me.'

'If it's about that ten per cent recovery fee . . . '

'You can have it. Just hear me out.'

'Go ahead,' Gillum said with a shrug.

'Last night Cole Devlin took my girl. I gotta turn that money over to him tonight or he'll — '

'It's too bad you won't be able to do that.'

'You can get the money back after he lets Diana go. Your company can afford the loss if something goes wrong!'

'But I can't,' Gillum said quietly. 'You see, Matt, the company and I had a parting of the ways shortly before you were released. And they know nothing about all this.' He was pleased by Matt's surprise. 'Now pick up that spade and dig yourself a nice comfortable grave.'

Matt hesitated, his insides twisting. Gillum cocked his pistol menacingly. The sound seemed magnified in the silence. Matt slowly picked up the spade. 'Might as well dig yours too, while I'm at it.'

'What's that supposed to mean?'

'You trailed me. You musta seen those Apache signs.'

'They were heading away from here. Now suppose you save your breath and dig.'

Matt began to dig. He took it slow, not wanting to tire himself too much. He'd already planted a worry seed in Gillum's mind, and with any luck he'd get jumpy and careless before the digging was done.

* * *

The sun had crawled past high noon and was scorching the earth with its furnace heat. Matt Sutton was dripping sweat, his shirt plastered to his back.

Digging, whether slow or quick, was a terrible exertion under the sun's fiery rays, and every spadeful of dirt sapped a little more of his remaining strength. He silently cursed this delay; if he didn't get a chance at Gillum soon he might not make it back to Bedlow before midnight. Of course, Gillum intended him to stay right here — permanently. He stopped, mopped a river of sweat from his eyes and forehead with a damp sleeve, and looked over at Gillum, sitting above him, his back against a wooden grave marker. The saddle-bags lay beside him and his six-gun was pointed directly at Matt's head, visible above the grave.

'That looks deep enough,' Gillum said casually. He stood and cautiously approached.

Matt quickly scooped up a loose spadeful of dirt, then lingered, spade in hand. 'Don't suppose it would do to appeal to your good nature?' he asked dryly.

'Not one little bit.' Gillum smiled

mirthlessly. 'Like I told you, nobody is to know about the money — and dead men can't carry tales.'

The silence was abruptly broken by a bird call. Matt froze, listening. The call was answered from another area. He felt his nape tingle. 'I said there shoulda been two graves.' Gillum tensed, listening, but not taking his eyes from Matt. ' 'Course, I'm the lucky one,' Matt drawled. 'You're gonna face 'em alone.' He grinned wickedly. 'Ever see a man after Apaches finished with him?'

'Shut up, Sutton,' Gillum snapped. A bird call came again, now closer. His head jerked in that direction.

This was what Matt had been waiting for. That split second of carelessness. He heaved the spadeful of dirt up into Gillum's face. Gillum staggered back, clawing at his face and firing a wild shot. Matt dropped the spade and scrambled up out of the grave.

Still blinded by dirt, Gillum tried to bring his gun to bear as he heard

Matt's charging footsteps. He was too late. Matt caught his wrist in both hands, and they grappled for the pistol. Gillum discharged another wild round, then began inching the muzzle toward Matt's face. Unable to force Gillum to drop the pistol, Matt desperately slammed a knee up into his groin as the muzzle was almost directly in front of his face. Gillum bellowed and sagged at the knees. Matt let loose a hand from Gillum's thick wrist and smashed him in the jaw.

Gillum reeled back against a grave marker that gave way and crashed to the ground with him. The six-gun flew from his hand and landed a few feet away. Matt lunged toward it, but Gillum recovered enough to thrust out a leg and trip him. Then he dragged himself up and, yanking a knife from under his coat, placed himself between Matt and the revolver.

Matt rolled to his feet and took a step forward only to be forced back by a vicious knife slash. Gillum was incredibly fast and agile for his years and weight, and his stabbing, thrusting blade made Matt continually give ground, backing him toward the open grave.

Suddenly Matt felt the crumbling edge of the grave beneath his boot heels and realized he couldn't retreat any further. Gillum lunged in low, aiming for the soft parts of his body, and Matt had no choice but to hurl himself backward to avoid being ripped open from groin to belly. He landed on his back, the fall jarring the air from his lungs. Then he saw Gillum's blurred shape looming above him.

Grinning victoriously, Gillum raised the knife and leaped down, straight at Matt.

Matt rolled aside, grabbed the spade and thrust it up at Gillum. He felt a rush of air as the knife sank into the ground beside his ear, and simultaneously felt a jolting impact against the spade.

With a long, agonized groan Gillum

awkwardly rolled off Matt and sagged against a side of the grave. His eyes went wide in horror and disbelief at the sight of the spade protruding from his stomach. Slowly his hands raised and his trembling fingers hesitantly closed around the wooden shaft as if to confirm that it was actually there. Then, while Matt watched, he gave a tug and half of the spade's bloody head slid out from his belly. And with that effort, the life went out of him and he died, spewing up blood.

Matt grimaced, clambered to his feet, and weakly dragged himself from the grave. He stood catching his breath, then stumbled to the saddle-bags and leaned down to pick them up.

Suddenly an arrow thudded into one of the bulging pockets.

Matt spun to see two Apaches charging across the graveyard. The lead one held a knife, the other a bow. Both wore war paint, light, long-sleeved shirts, breechcloths and knee-high moccasins. And they were coming at him fast.

Turning back, Matt yanked the arrow from its pocket and hefted the heavy saddle-bags onto a shoulder, then made for Gillum's six-gun. Behind him the lead Apache's racing, muffled footfalls bore down swiftly, filling his ears. Slowed by the weight of the saddle-bags, Matt grimly realized there was no hope of reaching the pistol in time. The Indian's shadow, knife arm raised, was already merging with his.

Shucking the saddle-bags, Matt grabbed a thick wooden marker and, ripping it from the ground, whirled, swinging upward with both hands. The flat wood crashed into the Indian's face and chest and he went down like a pole-axed steer. Matt raised the wood high and brought one end down on the Apache's skull, splitting it open. Then his eyes went to the second Apache who was approaching hard.

Dropping the marker, Matt swerved and made a long reaching dive for the pistol. His grasping hand closed around the gun's polished handle just as the second Apache's shadow fell over him. Matt rolled onto his back and fired up blindly. The round tore the Apache's flat, hard face apart and violently hurled him backward. He slammed to the ground, spreadeagled, raising dust.

Matt leaped up, ran back and collected the saddlebags, then headed to the sorrel who was stamping the ground nervously. He slung the saddlebags over the pommel and swung up in the saddle.

Distant war cries and hoofbeats shattered the tense quiet.

Startled, Matt looked past the cemetery and saw four Apaches charging out from a group of rocks. He wheeled the sorrel and, pistol in hand, galloped back to town. As he raced down the middle of the street an Apache suddenly stepped out from an alley and cut loose with a single-shot carbine. The slug shattered the sorrel's skull and it crashed to the ground, partly pinning

Matt's leg beneath it as it kicked in its death-throes. Matt dazedly sat up, saw the Apache fumbling to reload, and drew a bead on him.

The bullet ripped through the Apache's chest and knocked him sprawling back into the alley.

Hearing the pursuing Apaches growing nearer, Matt frantically kicked at the saddle with his free leg until he managed to dislodge his pinned one. He tore the saddle-bags loose from the saddle, slung them across one shoulder and ran to the opposite side of the street. He'd seen tracks of eight riders. Three were down, four were chasing him — that left one unaccounted for.

A horse's frightened whinny came from an alley ahead. Gripping the six-gun, Matt edged along the front of the building toward the alley, certain he'd find the missing Apache there. Reaching the corner he paused. A man's low, guttural voice was heard trying to calm the whinnying, stamping horse. Matt quietly cocked the pistol and stepped around the corner.

Back turned, the Apache stood clinging to the reins of Gillum's horse and trying to bring it under control. He heard Matt's movements and whirled, a hand going to a pistol in his belt. Matt quickly shot him through the throat, severing his jugular vein, and the Apache fell to the dirt. The reins tore free from his limp fingers as the pinto, anxious to escape the smell of blood, blindly bolted toward Matt. Waving his arms and shouting, Matt stepped into the middle of the narrow alley and stopped the frightened horse. He caught the dragging reins as the pinto reared and wrestled it under control. Then he heaved himself up into the saddle.

The four Apaches tore into town as Matt rode out into the street. He snapped off a hasty shot that slowed them for an instant and galloped away. The pistol was empty, but there was a Winchester in the saddle holster. He crouched low in the saddle as rifle and pistol fire whined and slapped around his head.

Breaking free from town well ahead of his pursuers, Matt raced the pinto toward the boulder-strewn hill where he'd make a stand. The pinto was fresher than the sorrel had been and he covered the distance in no time. He let the horse pick its way up into the rocks, then jerked the rifle from its scabbard and dismounted.

The howling Apaches were almost to the hill. Matt knew that he had to kill them all — and now. Leave even one alive to dog his trail and chances were he'd never reach Bedlow alive. He wanted them to keep right on coming so he took aim at the last man and squeezed off a shot.

The Apache was hit and somersaulted backward off his horse. The others continued on, unaware that the bullet had found its target.

Matt took careful aim again and picked off the third rider. The remaining two kept on with a vengeance, shrieking and firing, and were almost to the rocks. Matt couldn't allow that to happen. A deadly battle of stealth among the rocks would mean a costly delay — maybe even his life. He desperately began pumping rifle fire at them as fast as he could cock the Winchester.

A horse went down screaming; its rider tumbled across the ground, came up to his knees — only to be hit and hurled back down to stay. The last rider started up the hill, ran into a wall of rapid fire and fell, leaking like a sieve. As the sound of the last shot faded, Matt slowly lowered his rifle and solemnly surveyed the carnage below. Not a man moved, all remained sprawled in awkward postures of violent, unexpected death. His expression didn't change as his gaze ranged from one Apache to the next. Satisfied that none would get up and come at him again, he turned and moved to the waiting pinto.

Matt jammed the rifle back into its scabbard, then took the canteen from the saddle and unscrewed its cap. Gillum had used the water sparingly, and the canteen was over half full. He took a couple of thirsty gulps, then forced himself to lower the canteen. There was still a long, hard ride ahead and he and the pinto would need every drop before it was done. Matt replaced the canteen, hauled himself into the saddle and headed up the hill.

★ ★ ★

The sun hung like a brass ball in a blazing yellow sky. The still air shimmered with suspended heat, reflecting back off the desert floor.

Matt Sutton cursed silently and rolled a pebble around in his mouth to keep it from going dry. It was an old Indian trick he'd learned back in West Texas when he was little more than a boy. Seemed like fate, or whatever, was sure doing its damned best to stop him. The delays with Gillum and the Apaches had cost him any hope of reaching Bedlow before time for the meeting with Cole Devlin. And the way things looked he was gonna be lucky to be there by midnight.

Matt patted the saddle-bags draped over the pommel. Regret dug at him like a sharp stick. He'd never meant for Diana to get mixed up in all this. The money was meant to start them on a new life. That's all he'd thought about in prison. He'd never taken into consideration that something like this mess would happen. Gillum had sure been right when he'd called him a man pursued. With $50,000 of stolen money that's exactly what he was. And anyone he loved was in danger of becoming a tool to be used against him. Now it was up to him to get Diana back safe. Then he'd deal with Cole Devlin.

His thoughts as bleak as the wasteland he was travelling, he pushed the pinto into a canter and headed for the shade of the lengthening shadows from a group of rugged foothills.

8

Jenny Taylor and Emmet Wade sat in silence at a back table, ignoring the miners and cowboys who were whooping it up with the saloon girls to a lively tune provided by the piano player. She took a sip from the glass before her. This time her drink was real whiskey and not tea. She grimaced, almost choking on the strong liquor, and wrinkled her nose. She rarely drank, but tonight she felt a great need for something to calm her jittery nerves. Emmet didn't notice her reaction, he was too busy checking his silver-plated pocket watch for about the hundredth time.

'Looking at it won't make the time pass any faster,' she said, with a strained lightness. He nodded, forced a smile, but left the watch open on the table. Their eyes held briefly, each silently trying to reassure the other that things would go as planned, then the two returned to their own private thoughts.

Time crawled by on stumped legs.

Once more, Jenny felt guilty about her part in all this. Last night she could rationalize away her small part in Diana's kidnapping, but tonight she was to play an active part in Cole Devlin's plans. She didn't like it one bit; still, she couldn't fault his logic. It would buy more time for everyone to escape, even though it meant more hardship for Diana. She felt bad about that, but it couldn't be helped. And Devlin had promised Diana would be released unharmed.

Jenny took another drink of the strong whiskey to clear her mind, then smiled across the table at Emmet and asked, 'What time is it?'

* * *

It was 11.30 according to Jack Rath's expensive gold watch. He returned it to a vest pocket, then checked the feel of the double holsters on his hips. Usually he left the gunplay to Rio and the others, but tonight $50,000 was at stake. For that kind of money he was willing to risk swapping a little lead. He wasn't as fast as a professional gunfighter, but he was an accurate shot. He'd learned to shoot as a boy, not on the frontier but on his family's Long Island estate.

Rath smiled, wondering what his blue-blood relations would say when the black sheep returned hale, hearty and prosperous. He was certain they were all picturing him living in squalor, or as a permanent fixture in one of the country's many houses of correction.

There was a knock at the back door. Rath took his hat and answered it. Rio was standing at the top of the stairs.

'Norton, Ike and Spence are waiting down below,' the laconic gunman informed him.

'Fine,' Rath said, stepping outside. 'We'll take a leisurely stroll over to the stock pens.' He turned and locked the door. 'And come back just a *little* richer than when we started.' For once Rio's smile didn't appear pained. He stepped aside and Rath led the way down the stairs to where Norton and two other hardcases stood waiting.

★ ★ ★

Diana Logan and the three men rode slowly alongside the railroad tracks toward the stock pens and a cluster of buildings and boxcars ahead. They rode cautiously, the men's eyes searching the shadows for signs of an ambush. Diana was gagged, a knotted bandanna thrust between her teeth, deeply into her mouth, her wrists tied to the saddle horn and her ankles fastened to the stirrups. Jesse was leading her horse at the rear of the group. She had no fear that Matt wouldn't be there, and tensed expectantly as a figure separated itself from the shadows between two buildings ahead, past the pens crowded with sleeping cattle.

The group drew up warily, Cole's hand going to his gun butt while Shank raised the Winchester draped across his saddle. The figure waved, stepped further out into the moonlight, and was recognized as Emmet Wade. The men relaxed and pushed their horses across the tracks.

The group reined up before Emmet, and Cole asked, 'Is everythin' all set?'

'Yeah,' Emmet answered. 'There ain't no sign of Sutton yet.'

Cole took a watch from a pocket of his black shirt and checked it in the moonlight. 'He's still got twenty minutes to go. Let's git outa sight.'

They rode around the side of the building and the men climbed down from their saddles and stretched. Diana sat waiting, but no one made a move to untie her from her horse. Disturbed by the group's arrival the cattle began milling about in the pens.

'Next time any of them critters comes West,' Cole commented, 'it'll be as cans of corned beef.' He turned to Emmet and asked, 'Well, where is she?' Emmed turned and beckoned into the shadows.

Diana turned her head at the nearby sound of rustling fabric and saw Jenny Taylor, wearing her short, low-cut, red, dance-hall dress, hesitantly emerge from the shadows. She took small satisfaction that the girl was unable to look her in the eye. Diana sat seething. If she weren't tightly tied and gagged she would not only tell the girl a thing or two, she'd do her best to scratch her eyes out!

'Well now, ain't you somethin' to look at?' Devlin said, grinning from ear to ear, as Jenny moved to Emmet's side. She smiled wanly and huddled against him for comfort. Smiling paternally, Devlin placed his bony hands on Emmet and Jenny's shoulders and spoke to them in a low, confidential tone.

Diana couldn't hear what was being said, but Devlin's straying gaze made it clear they were discussing her. And her fear returned with a vengeance.

* * *

Across the open plain, Matt Sutton saw the lights of Bedlow ahead and pushed the failing pinto into a gallop. Time was short and he had to get there — even if it meant riding the horse into the ground. Nothing must keep him from reaching the stock pens by midnight.

* * *

Deputies Billy Clark and Yance Boyne were making their late-night rounds along Main Street, pausing to check store doors and peer into the dark alleys. So far things were nice and quiet, except for the goings on inside the saloons and bawdy-houses. Yance liked it like that. But Billy had had a burr under his saddle even worse than usual ever since Matt Sutton hit

town. The fact that they hadn't seen
Sutton since his arrival only made
things worse. Yance surely hoped he
wasn't anywhere around when Clark
did get his chance at Sutton. True,
he'd give a pretty penny to see Clark
taken down, but he sure as hell didn't
want to be the one who'd have to arrest
Sutton afterwards.

The deputies reached the end of the
block and started to amble across the
street. Suddenly they heard a galloping
horse tearing along the dark cross street
and skedaddled across to the opposite
corner with no time to spare. The
horseman turned onto Main Street and
kept right on going without looking
back.

'Wonder where's he's a-goin' in such
a hurry?' Yance asked.

Billy Clark's jaw dropped as he stared
after the rider. 'That's Sutton – on Mr
Gillum's horse!'

'So?' Yance said. 'It appears like he's
bringin' 'im back.'

'Something is going on. He's riding

like the devil was at his coat-tails.'
Yance shrugged. Billy hitched up his
double-holstered gunbelt. 'I'm gonna
follow him. You go wake Sheriff
Keeler.'

'The hell I will,' Yance exclaimed,
well aware of the sheriff's reaction if
he was dragged out of bed for nothing.
But Billy Clark was already pounding
along the boardwalk as fast as his
bandy legs would carry him. Yance
shook his head in disgust. The little
hellion was bent on finding trouble, so
let him. Seeing as Sutton's guns were
locked up in the office, the most he'd
do would be to kick the hell outa Clark.
Yance smiled, relishing the thought.
That sure wasn't worth rousting Keeler
outa his nice warm bed over. Besides,
just who the all-fired hell did Clark
think he was to be giving orders? *He*
was the senior deputy here, not him!

Holding that thought, Yance Boyne
turned and continued on his rounds.

★ ★ ★

As Matt neared the stock pen area, the gasping pinto, every hair on its body stiff with sweat, stumbled. He yanked its head up and the horse staggered a few more yards. Then it gave out and sank to the ground on all fours, too exhausted to rise. Matt stepped down, grabbed the saddle-bags and, slinging them across one shoulder, took off in a weary run, leaving the pinto there in the middle of the street.

There was no time to waste checking his watch, he knew it was about midnight – and he was going to be late.

★ ★ ★

Chewing on the butt of a lean cigar, Cole Devlin stood leaning against the corner of the building where his group waited in the shadows. He checked his watch.

It was exactly midnight.

Cole scowled and put the watch away. Maybe it was a mite fast. Ole

Matt was an honourable man. His word was his bond and he'd never go back on it. 'Sides, he was in love, and he sure wouldn't chance anythin' happenin' to that beautiful, yellow-haired woman of his.

'See 'im yet, Cole?' Jesse whispered, from around the corner.

'Nope,' Cole answered easily.

'It's done past midnight,' Shank growled impatiently. 'He ain't comin', so let's just shoot her and go.'

Cole saw Diana's large eyes widen fearfully over her gag as she sat tied on her horse, her riding cape removed. 'Now that's real bright, Shank,' he scolded. 'Then Sutton shows and we got us a dead woman to trade.'

'But I thought — ' Shank began.

Cole hushed him and turned back, listening, eyes stabbing at the darkness. He saw Matt Sutton's lean figure break from between two buildings about thirty yards down and stagger out into the moonlight. Cole took the cigar butt from his mouth, dropped it into a shirt pocket and called, 'Over here, Matt.' He unbuckled his gunbelt and handed it to Jesse.

'You loco?' Jesse asked in surprise. 'He might — '

'He ain't gonna start nothin' till after she's safe.' Holding his arms well out at his sides, Cole stepped out into the moonlight. 'You're late, Matt,' he chided. 'That's mighty poor manners.'

Lungs close to bursting, Matt staggered to one of the crowded cattle pens and braced a hand against a wooden rail for support. He fixed his eyes on Devlin's moonlit figure standing away from the corner of a building, a safe distance away. He wasn't wearing a gun, but that didn't mean the others didn't have him in their sights. It took a few more deep gasps before Matt was able to send his voice any distance. He held up the saddle-bags for Devlin to see.

'I . . . got your money, Devlin. Where's Diana?'

'She's right here,' Devlin called

pleasantly, 'all bright-eyed and bushy-tailed.' He turned and gestured to someone around the corner. A couple of long moments dragged by, then Diana's nervous voice called, 'Matt . . . Matt' I'm all right . . . they — '

Matt tensed as her voice abruptly broke off, muffled into silence. 'Devlin . . . ' he began.

'You heard her for yourself,' Devlin interrupted. 'Now bring the saddle-bags closer, then toss 'em this way as hard as you can and back off. Soon as you do, I'll send her out.'

Matt hesitated warily. He still didn't trust Devlin, especially whenever his voice took on that 'good old buddy' tone. He'd seen him use it too many times in prison to throw somebody off their guard and then strike like a coiled rattler. But there wasn't much else he could do; he had failed to make it back in time to form any plans of his own. And in his mad haste to get here he'd even left the rifle in its saddle holster when he'd abandoned the exhausted pinto in the middle of the street.

'I'm waitin', Matt,' Devlin called, a mild edge to his voice, 'and so's your girl.'

Matt slowly started forward along the line of cattle pens, his eyes darting between Devlin's black-clad figure and the corner of the building.

When he'd covered a little better than half the distance separating them, Devlin called sharply, 'That's far enough, Matt. Pitch it here and then git on back a'ways.'

Matt reluctantly heaved the saddle-bags. They plopped to the ground heavily, stirring dust, a few yards in front of him, near the shadows of the building. Muscles coiled springs, he began edging away, ready to bolt forward at the first hint of a double-cross. When Devlin was satisfied that an equal distance separated them from the saddle-bags he turned and beckoned.

'Awright, bring her out.'

Matt stiffened, his eyes going expectantly to the corner of the building. He was surprised to see that Devlin had a third member in his gang: the young man in the yellow shirt who'd been talking with the saloon girl he'd mistaken for Diana. He stepped out into the moonlight with Diana, who stood partly in the shadows. The hood of her riding cape was back, revealing her swirling blonde hair, but the lower part of her face was concealed by a wide cloth gag. Her hands were tied together in front of her, and her fingers nervously clutched the cape closed so that little more than a bit of one long black-stockinged leg could be seen. Yellow Shirt nodded and gently prodded her forward. Spine rigid, she advanced slowly and stiffly, keeping partly in the shadows.

'You see, Matt,' Devlin called, pleased with himself, 'I'm a man of my word.'

Matt didn't bother to reply, his eyes were on Diana and Yellow Shirt, who stood there watching her slow progress. She had probably been warned to take it slow, just in case he had some smart move planned to try and regain both her and the saddle-bags. She drew even with the saddle-bags and hesitated. Her head swivelled to them, less than a dozen steps away. Matt knew what she was thinking. No, don't risk it, he urged mentally. He'd get them back himself later.

Abruptly, Diana slipped her hands free from the rope and, one end dangling from her slim wrist, ran to the saddle-bags. She scooped them up, then whirled and, cape flying behind her, ran back toward Yellow Shirt.

'Diana,' Matt shouted, confused, taking a step forward.

Pulling the cloth down from her mouth with her free hand, she threw a frightened glance back at him. For the first time her white face was caught fully by the brilliant moonlight.

It was the blonde girl from the saloon.

'Devlin, you bastard!' Matt yelled,

recovering from the surprise and charging forward at the same time Devlin ran to meet the girl.

'Hold it!' a voice called sharply, cracking the silence like a rifle shot.

Matt, Devlin and the blonde halted, whirling in the direction of the voice.

Slowly five shapes moved out from the line of boxcars and approached. They stopped partly in the moonlight, and Matt recognized Jack Rath and his four gunmen.

'Well, well . . . if it isn't Jenny Taylor,' Rath remarked sardonically. 'I dislike my employees trying to steal from me.' Jenny stared at him blankly and stood clutching the saddle-bags to her breast, like a small child clinging protectively to her doll. Rath holstered one six-gun and held out his hand. He smiled, but his voice was utterly chilled. 'Bring the saddle-bags here . . . please.' Jenny needed no urging; she'd heard that tone before in his voice, and made haste to obey.

Seeing that Rath and his men's eyes

were on Jenny and the saddle-bags, Matt carefully edged back toward the stock-pen gate. He noticed Yellow Shirt fade into the shadows and disappear around the corner of the building.

'Ain't it a caution,' Devlin remarked ruefully, his eyes following Jenny, who was passing near him on her way to Rath. 'Here, a man works hard to git somethin', and some other fella up and takes it away.'

'You Southern trash should be used to losing by now,' Rath commented dryly. 'Isn't that right, Sutton?'

Matt halted as unwanted attention was called to him.

'Matt, you gonna let this here damn yankee talk to *you* that way?' Devlin asked, incredulously.

Matt remained silent, aware that Devlin was attempting to stall and direct attention away from himself. One long leap and he'd have the gate open, bringing confusion to all as the packed cattle burst free. But, without

135

a diversion he'd have more holes in him than a prairie dog village before he could reach it.

Then came an unexpected diversion.

Deputy Billy Clark rushed out from between two buildings. 'Hey, what's going on there, Sutton?' he shouted, both hands going to his holsters as he ran toward the group.

Rio pivoted and, with casual ease, flipped up his pistol and fired.

Before Billy's guns cleared their holsters something exploded violently in his chest. His arms went wide in a vain effort to support himself against the emptiness around him as he gulped air for a long, agonizing moment of stunned disbelief. Then the ear-shattering crack of the six-gun filled his ears and he was abruptly on the ground, dust swirling about him, with his face pressed into earth that stank of cattle urine and manure. And pain came, at last. His trembling lips silently mouthing the word 'Ma', Billy Clark flopped over on to his back and lay still, his blood staining the dirt, his wide, sightless eyes staring up at the full moon dominating the night sky.

Then all hell broke loose.

9

The air rang with gunfire and rebel yells as Cole Devlin's bunch came charging around the corner of a building. Shank led Devlin's horse and Matt tensed at the sight of Diana, in her brief black costume, gagged and tied on a horse led by Jesse. Then came the kid in the yellow shirt. The frightened cattle added their bawling to the pandemonium.

Caught by surprise, Rath and his men fell back toward the boxcars, firing as they went. Eyes wild with terror and confusion, Jenny Taylor stood rooted to the spot hugging the saddle-bags.

Matt leaped to the gate, threw back the crossbar and dragged it open, loosing a stream of head-tossing steers. Shielded by the gate, he stood watching as the mass of snorting cattle scattered in all directions, slowing the surprised horsemen.

As his horse reached him, Devlin grabbed the pommel with both hands and hauled himself into the saddle, narrowly avoiding being trampled by a blatting steer.

Emmet was making for Jenny when a slug caught him high in the right side of his chest. He swayed, but managed to cling to the saddle horn and kept from falling to certain death beneath the hoofs of stampeding cattle.

Dodging bullets and cattle, Rath and his men retreated into the relative safety of an open boxcar.

Devlin forced his horse through the knot of cattle to Jenny who was trying to reach the side of the empty pen. She saw him and frantically held out her hands to him, one clutching the saddle-bags, imploringly. Leaning down, Devlin snatched the saddle-bags from her hand as he rode by. Jenny screamed tearfully after him but he kept riding.

Rath fired after Devlin, then turned

to Norton. 'Get Jenny. We need her!' The big man looked out at Jenny, clinging to the fence as steers rushed around her, then back at Rath as though he'd taken leave of his senses. 'Damn it, man, move!' Rath roared, nearly apoplectic. Norton opened his mouth to argue. A strong shove from Rath abruptly ended any discussion and sent him sprawling from the boxcar. Norton scrambled up and, firing his six-gun in the air, began making his way through the veering steers to Jenny.

Matt broke from behind the gate as Devlin started past, slowed by the milling cattle, and leaped up to drag him from the saddle. But Devlin was ready. A boot heel kicked solidly against Matt's forehead, sending him flying backward. He hit the ground hard and rolled. Devlin rode on, broke free of the cattle, and raced to join the rest of his gang.

Weak and dazed, Matt dragged himself to the tracks and into the shadows beneath a boxcar as he heard Rath and his men leave their shelter and fire after Devlin.

Norton stood twisting one of Jenny's arms behind her back as she sobbed and struggled. The last steers were ploughing their way out on to the open plain when Rath and the three other men joined Norton and Jenny. Rath eyed the sobbing blonde coldly, then shifted his gaze to Norton.

'You and Ike take Jenny up the back stairs to my office. She has quite a bit of talking to do.'

'No!' Jenny screamed in a display of defiance and increased her struggles. Ike jerked the loosely hanging cloth up from her neck and roughly shoved it between her lips. Norton caught her other arm, tugged it behind her and, using the rope still dangling from one slim wrist, tied her hands. The men adjusted her cape to conceal her helplessness and dragged her off between them.

Rath turned to Spence. 'Get our

horses and have them waiting behind the saloon.' The gunman nodded and moved away. Rath then directed a thoughtful eye to Billy Clark's trampled body. 'Rio, we're going to find Sheriff Keeler and, being honest, upright citizens, tell him that Matt Sutton killed a deputy.'

From underneath the boxcar, Matt, his vision blurred by the agony ripping through his head from Devlin's kick, lay watching the two men leave. Soon the place would be swarming with curious and outraged citizens. He had to get away, clear his head and think straight. The only way he could find Devlin was through Jenny Taylor – and that meant first getting her away from Rath and his gunmen. A tall order.

Painfully Matt crawled out on the other side of the tracks and then stumbled his way along the line of boxcars.

* * *

Pounding hoofbeats roused Rose from her worried thoughts and sent her eagerly to the cabin door. She flung it open and, framed by the light spilling through the doorway, stood squinting into the darkness. Relief flooded through her as she recognized Cole's lean figure at the head of the group crossing the moonlit clearing. Joyfully she waved and called to him. He whooped and galloped toward her. She ran out to meet him.

'Cole, I'm sure glad you're back safe!' she cried breathlessly as he reined his horse before her.

'Why the hell shouldn't I be?' He grinned and stepped down.

'Did you git it?' Rose asked anxiously.

He nodded and patted the bulging saddle-bags. 'Right here.' Rose gave a pleased cry, threw her arms around his neck and kissed him, long and hard. To her disappointment his response was lukewarm and impatient. He disengaged himself and stepped back. 'That'll hafta keep a spell.'

Rose frowned, slightly hurt and bewildered. Cole hadn't even noticed her new hair-do. Hoping to please him, she'd emulated the white-girl's style and her raven hair, painstakingly combed and brushed to a sheen, was now parted on the side and hung loose, almost masking one eye. Then she saw Jesse come up leading a horse and grimly understood Cole's indifference. The tall, golden-haired girl sat tied and gagged on the horse. Her cape was gone and her splendid, scantily clad body was revealed for all to see — particularly Cole! The sight incensed Rose.

'What's she doin' back here?' she demanded. Cole ignored her, lifted down the saddle-bags and swung them over his shoulder. Rose's temper continued to flare. 'You said we'd be rid of her as soon as you got the money!'

'Somethin' went wrong,' Cole snapped defensively. 'We still need her.' He turned to Jesse who'd dismounted and was untying the captive from her horse.

'Put the horses in the barn, but leave 'em saddled.'

'Right,' Jesse responded, not looking round. As the ropes fell away from her wrists, Diana reached up and hastily drew the bandanna down from her mouth, letting it hang about her neck, and breathed a relieved sigh. Then she sat rubbing her aching wrists while Jesse freed her ankles.

'Cole, are you gonna drag her around the rest of your life?' Rose shouted, stamping a booted foot and gesturing.

Roughly Cole caught Rose's waving arm, jerked her around and pointed to Shank who was helping Emmet from his saddle. 'Can't you see we got us a wounded man?' he demanded hotly. Rose's anger waned on seeing the wide crimson stain soaking the middle of Emmet's yellow shirt and hearing him groan with every step as the big man gently supported him into the cabin. She turned apologetically to Cole and started to speak, but he interrupted, 'Now hush up and start pullin' with me, woman!' She nodded meekly. He turned her to face Diana as Jesse helped her down from her mount. 'You wanna do somethin' useful, bring her inside and tie her good while I see to Emmet.' He gave her a none-too-gentle push forward, then turned and stomped toward the cabin.

Rose stared after Cole, then turned bitter eyes upon her hated rival. The white girl stood rubbing her wrists and glancing about, uncertain, as Jesse moved off with the horses. Go on, make a break for it, Rose mentally urged as she stalked up to Diana, hoping for an excuse to vent her anger on her. But Diana just stood there. Rose seized one of Diana's wrists and wrenched it up behind her back. Diana gave a sharp gasp but made no effort to struggle as she was herded to the cabin.

Rose eased up on her roughness as they entered the cabin, but the men paid her no mind. Emmet was sitting on the side of a bunk while

Cole poured whiskey down his throat and Shank relieved him of his bloody shirt.

The women passed and were about to enter the back room, when Cole called, 'Soon's you finish with her, Rose, come on out and lend a hand while I do the cuttin'.'

Rose halted Diana in the doorway and looked back at him. 'Shouldn't we fetch a doctor?'

'The hell you say,' Cole rasped. 'We might as well bring the sheriff along, too!'

Shank nodded. 'That's right, Rose.'

Seeing that further talk was useless, Rose said, 'I'll be out directly,' and forced Diana into the back room. She kicked the door shut with her heel and gave Diana a hard shove that sent her reeling toward the bunk, then turned and took lengths of clothes' line from a nearby peg. 'Why'd you hafta come back?' she said, more to herself than Diana.

Standing before the bunk and rubbing

her pained wrist, Diana answered coolly, 'I didn't have a choice.'

'You coulda run away.'

Diana's large blue eyes widened incredulously. 'Tied on a horse?'

'I'd've done it,' Rose said flatly, though secretly she had her doubts.

'I'm not you.'

Bristling, Rose stalked to her and demanded, 'What's that supposed to mean?'

Aware that Rose was spoiling for an excuse to hurt her, Diana met her dark eyes evenly, then shrugged and said innocently, 'I don't know any Indian tricks.'

'All right,' Rose said, smiling tauntingly, 'I'm gonna teach you an Indian trick. Lie down on your stomach. Cross your ankles and put your hands behind your back.' Diana complied hesitantly and Rose leaned over her with the ropes.

* * *

Face set in a scowl of concentration, Cole Devlin carefully withdrew the flat-nosed slug from Emmet's bloody chest with his knife and fingers and dropped it to the floor. The tension drained from his face and he looked to Rose and the other two men who, until he'd finally fainted, had been holding Emmet down on the bunk. 'Bandage him up.'

'Will he be all right?' Rose asked, concerned.

'Depends,' Cole answered with a shrug. Then he turned to Shank. 'Git outside and keep watch.' The big man nodded, took his Winchester and went out.

'I still say he needs a doctor,' Rose insisted.

'We done discussed that, woman,' Cole snapped irritably.

Rose turned to Jesse for support. Not looking up from the sheet he was tearing, Jesse said quietly, 'If the kid's gonna pull through, Rose, he'll do it without any doctor.'

149

Leaving the two to tend the wounded man, Cole moved to the table, set the bloody knife down and ran a hand over the bulging saddle-bags. He pulled back a flap, removed a stack of bills and, grinning, slowly shifted his eyes to the other door. Then he stuffed the bills into a shirt pocket and headed for the back room.

Rose's demanding voice immediately halted him in his tracks, 'Where you goin', Cole?'

'To check on the girl,' he replied innocently.

'I tied her good — just like you said.'

Not wanting to argue, Cole eyed her for a moment in exasperation, then said, 'You just worry about bandaging him tight, so's he don't bleed to death after all my hard work.' He ignored her dark scowl and strode off.

Lying on her side, Diana watched Cole enter, closing the door behind him. 'I ain't gonna hurt you none,' he said soothingly. His words failed to melt her icy expression. He stood surveying the taut rows of rope looped about her torso, pinning her tied wrists and arms against her back, and the others around her knees and crossed ankles. Rose had sure done her job well. The blonde was secured in knots which only an Injun coulda tied.

'I just come to be friendly,' he said, sitting on the edge of the bed. Diana squirmed back, drawing her legs up as much as she was able. He leaned closer and rested a hand on her black-stockinged leg. She kicked, dug her high heels into his thigh and ground. Cole grunted, caught her ankles in one hand and held them as she struggled. He pulled a shoe from her foot, dropped it to the floor, then removed her remaining one. 'Seems like you're always tryin' to kill me with one of these,' he remarked, staring at the slender high heel. Diana made no reply. Carelessly he tossed the shoe over his shoulder, to land at the foot of the bunk, and moved nearer.

Her back against the wall, Diana stopped struggling and glared up at him coldly. Her only defence was aloof silence. She must not, at whatever cost, acknowledge her helplessness.

'You don't fool me,' Cole said, taking the bills from his pocket and holding them before Diana's frigid face. 'This here's why you was stickin' with Sutton.' He caressed her bare shoulder lightly, felt her tense at his touch. 'Now I'm willin' to share this with you. We could have a lotta good times . . . see a lotta places.' His hand moved up, traced the contour of her cheek. 'What do you say?'

Diana shifted her gaze and stared past him impassively. To put her scorn into words might ignite the powder keg of Devlin's emotions. Though she could feel rather than see his dark eyes raking over her, she didn't blink or move a single muscle as she lay enduring his touch.

'I ain't half bad,' Cole cajoled, 'once you git to know me.' His hand moved to her hair, idly twirled a long golden lock between his fingers. 'Take Rose — she hated me at first when I shot her Injun husband and carried her off.' He laughed, amused. 'Now she can't do without me.' He dropped the money on the bunk, took her shoulders and drew her up to him. Diana didn't resist, continued staring off. 'You'll be just like her, too, if you give yourself a chance.' He lowered his head to hers and planted a coarse kiss on her carefully unmoving and unresponsive lips.

Diana let her body go limp, her head lolling backward, seeking to break the kiss. But Devlin persisted. She felt her lips mashed against her teeth as his lips ground painfully against her soft mouth, hard, possessive and bruising. She restrained a cry, didn't move or return his probing kiss and kept her large eyes open. It worked. After a moment, Devlin broke off the kiss and she saw the animal desire fade from his face as though she'd struck him.

'What in tarnation's wrong with you?' he demanded furiously. Diana stared up coolly, as if he weren't there. He shoved her away. She fell back on the bunk limply and lay motionless. Cole scowled down at her, then roughly grabbed a fistful of her hair. 'Don't just lie there lookin' at me. Say somethin' — anythin'!' With great effort Diana betrayed no emotion. He released her, snatched the bills and stood. 'Woman, you . . . you're squirrely!' he said in exasperation, pointing accusingly and waggling the bills before her. 'And that's a sure enough fact!' She stared through him. Cole turned and stomped toward the door, shaking his head.

On reaching the door, Cole regained his composure and looked back at Diana. 'You give my offer some serious thought, hear?' He might as well have been talking to a brick wall. Cole yanked the door open and almost collided with Rose, who was about to enter. 'Git outa the damn way,' he muttered and shouldered her aside.

Hurt, Rose stared after Cole sullenly, then stepped in and closed the door. She quietly drew the bolt shut then, levelling her stern gaze on Diana, slouched into the chair beside the door and drew her knife from its sheath.

Though Diana tried to appear indifferent, inwardly she feared Rose more than Devlin or his men. A jealous woman was irrational and impulsive. Rose was one mean, jealous woman. Her breath became a pain in her chest as she watched Rose eye her broodingly and toy with the sharp blade. She was aware of her utter helplessness and of the harsh cruelty of the knots Rose had tied. She was also aware that she mustn't break and reveal her fear to the half-breed girl who was awaiting any pretext, real or imagined, to put an end to her rival. And she knew she didn't trust herself to continue this staring match with Rose.

Lithe muscles straining hard, Diana gracelessly rolled over and faced the rough-hewn wall. She still felt Rose's cold, unblinking gaze and an icy ripple of fear crept down her body. She drew a calming breath and, fighting her growing desolation, tried to reassure herself that Matt was coming for her.

He must!

★ ★ ★

Cole and Jesse stood over Emmet as he groaned and began to stir. 'We can't leave him behind,' Jesse said.

'We got no choice,' Cole snorted. 'If we try to move him, he'll up and die on us for sure. And we can't stick around here for weeks waitin' on him to git better.' He shrugged and added, ' 'Sides, his girl will look after him.'

'Yeah, but somebody oughta stay and help her.'

'Somebody will,' Cole said quietly, throwing a sly look at the back room. He moved to the table, sat and began taking the money from the saddle-bags. Jesse ambled up and gave the money his full attention, leaving Emmet to ramble about Jenny Taylor as her distorted image danced in his fever-addled mind.

The wounded youth was unaware that, despite her own pain, Jenny's thoughts were on him at that same moment.

10

The phonograph filled Rath's apartment with a lilting Strauss waltz, sharply contrasting the ugly scene as Norton's vicious slap brought another anguished cry from Jenny Taylor's bruised mouth.

Comfortably settled in his easy chair, Jack Rath idly watched the smoke rings from his glowing cheroot drift toward the ceiling. He wasn't squeamish but, unlike Norton and Rio, he took no delight in the sufferings of a beautiful woman. Why in hell was the girl so obstinate? Then he remembered the youth in the yellow shirt and smiled as he answered his own question. She was a woman in love. No matter how meek she appeared, such a woman was capable of a fierce inner strength when her loved one was threatened.

'That's enough,' he commanded curtly, halting the bearded man as he drew back his brawny arm to strike the helpless girl again. 'This is taking far too long. It's time we tried a different way.' He blew another smoke ring, then studied the smouldering tip of his cigar. The two men watched him curiously, waiting for his next order. Rath's eyes moved thoughtfully to the blonde girl slumped limply against the many ropes holding her in the chair, head drooped on to a bare shoulder, long, dishevelled hair obscuring her battered face. Then he called Norton to him and held out the cigar. As the burly man approached, grinning sadistically, Rath looked to Rio, who stood behind Jenny's chair, and said pointedly, 'See that she's not too loud.'

Jenny moaned and weakly tried to turn her head aside as Rio pulled up the loose bandanna to her mouth and forced it between her teeth. Her pain-blurred eyes saw Norton returning, holding the burning cigar before him like a torch, and she gasped and recoiled against the chair's hard wooden back.

Relishing her fear, Norton stopped before Jenny and gently blew on the cheroot's tip, which glowed redly inside its long grey ash. His taunting grin widened as he watched her desperately tug at her ropes, her head lolling back and forth as muffled, uncontrollable mewling sounds escaped her gag and mingled with the lovely, swaying waltz music.

'You just nod when you feel like talking about something interesting, you hear?' he said, almost kindly, and plunged the cigar down on one of her sharply drawn-back shoulders.

Jenny's prolonged, muted shriek nearly succeeded in drowning out the phonograph.

★ ★ ★

Torches sputtering in the wind, mounted men galloped up and down the main street while other torch-bearing groups on foot stalked the narrow, winding side streets, all hunting Matt Sutton. Despite the seriousness of their task, a festive air prevailed as the self-important bands invaded homes and businesses, especially the whorehouses and cribs on Walker Street, in search of the fugitive. There hadn't been so much excitement since last spring when the two Bodine brothers were hanged for rustling. Nobody seemed to worry that one careless torch could turn the whole town into a blazing inferno.

From the roof of McCulley's General Store, Matt Sutton watched the frenetic activity below and fretted about how he was going to reach the Cut and Shoot Saloon a block away, on the other side of the wide main street. There was no doubt that Jenny Taylor would be 'persuaded' to reveal the location of Cole Devlin's hide-out. He only hoped he could get her away from Rath before she broke. Matt wormed his way back from the roof's edge as a boisterous group came along the boardwalk, their torches casting long distorted shadows.

As he lay listening to their passing footsteps, a plan came to him. He might not be able to travel the streets, but he could travel the rooftops. Grudging the delay, he waited until the men were well down the street and then, crouched low, sneaked to the side of the roof and looked across at the next rooftop. It was about six feet away. He moved back, listened. No one was heard on the boardwalk. He charged across the roof and hurled himself into space.

Matt landed heavily on the next roof and froze. No startled voices came from below, so if there were any living-quarters inside the building they must be in the back. He moved across the roof and, with cougar-like grace, began making his way across the rooftops.

★ ★ ★

Slender fingers flexing and clawing the air wildly, as a muffled half-scream, half-sob tore from her raw throat, Jenny Taylor arched her body in the chair, which shook and rattled madly beneath her. The cheroot's fiery touch had long since become unbearable. Her mind and body screamed for relief. Please, God, let Emmet forgive me! she prayed, as her head, hanging back over the chair, violently bobbed in submission.

Rio quickly stepped to Norton's side and grabbed his thick wrist, jerking the cheroot away from Jenny's scorched flesh. 'Damn it, she's ready to talk,' he hissed. 'Quit that or she'll pass out on us again!' The bearded man scowled his disappointment and reluctantly moved away. Rio gently raised Jenny's head. 'You *are* gonna talk at us, ain't you, sugar?' he asked pointedly. She stared up at him with pain-dulled eyes and managed a feeble nod. He untied her gag and, hating her weakness and blaming her love for not being strong enough to withstand her suffering, Jenny reluctantly let the words spill out between piteous sobs.

* * *

Matt Sutton stood in a dark alley and stared across the street at the Cut and Shoot Saloon as a drunk wandered out, swaying and clutching a bottle, watching a group of possemen disappear around a corner. Giving a disgusted wave, the drunk staggered down the steps and weaved toward several horses tied to a hitching post near the alley. Matt tensed expectantly; this was the break he needed. He smiled tightly as the drunk unsuccessfully tried to avoid a pile of fresh horse droppings in the middle of the street. While the man was distracted, cussing and awkwardly wiping his boot in the dirt, silently Matt broke from the alley and made for the hitching rail.

Matt ducked down between the rail and the water trough and waited. The drunk shambled up to a bay tied between two other horses and, bracing a hand against its hindquarters, laboriously worked his way toward the stirrup. Reaching his goal, he fumbled with the stirrup and attempted to mount. Matt sprang up, jerked the man around and clipped him on the jaw. The drunk dropped his bottle and collapsed into his arms.

After stripping the drunk of his hat and coat, Matt rolled him under the boardwalk, then untied the bay and, clutching the bottle to his chest, led it toward an alley on one side of the saloon. Resisting the impulse to hurry, he kept his head down and carefully imitated the drunk's stumbling walk. As he neared the saloon, two men came out and paused in conversation. Matt stopped and made a pretence of drunkenly adjusting the horse's bridle while silently damning the drunk for not carrying a gun. Locked in conversation, the men turned and moved away. Matt drew a relieved breath, led the horse on and entered the alley.

At the back of the saloon Matt left the bay tied to the railing and crept up Rath's private stairs. As he neared the landing he heard music coming from inside the apartment. He moved to the door and listened. No voices were heard, but that didn't mean he might not be walking into a roomful of guns. He hooked a leg over the railing, leaned out and grabbed the window sill.

Peering under the shade, drawn to within an inch from the bottom of the window, Matt saw Jenny Taylor awkwardly slouched in a chair, held in place by a multitude of ropes. She seemed to be alone in the dimly lit room. He pushed himself away from the window and returned to the door. Trying to make as little noise as possible, Matt put his shoulder against the door. It gave way on his second try.

He stepped inside, poised to attack or retreat, and threw a sweeping glance about the room. Jenny was alone. Closing the door, he strode over to her and whispered her name. She didn't respond. He touched her shoulder gently. She gave a small jerk, emitted a muffled groan. He untied her gag and put his lips close to her ear.

'Jenny, do you hear me?' She whimpered but didn't raise her head from her breast. Then she murmured something, but the phonograph drowned her words.

Matt went to the machine and stood trying to figure out how to turn it off. He grabbed the cylinder and pulled. The music stopped abruptly as it came free and broke in his hand. He picked up the low-burning lamp beside the machine and returned to Jenny. As the light fell over her, he winced at the sight of what the bastards had done.

As well as bruises on her face, the tears in her dress revealed round, angry, red burns vividly contrasting with her pale skin. The girl had taken a helluva lot of punishment, and he couldn't fault her if she'd broken. That was what he had to find out – fast.

Setting the lamp on the floor by her black-stockinged foot, lashed at the slim ankle to a side rung of the chair, Matt gently raised her chin and turned her to him.

'Please, Mr Rath,' she whimpered, her voice barely audible, 'don't let him hurt me any more . . . I told the truth.'

'Jenny, it's Matt Sutton.' She squinted up at him through groggy, slitted eyes, then gasped as a flicker of recognition crossed her face. 'I'm not gonna hurt you,' Matt said softly. 'I want to help.' Her fear became desperation. Matt pushed his face closer as she forced the words from her throat with great difficulty.

'Stop him . . . he'll kill Emmet . . . kill them all . . . wants the money . . . didn't want to tell . . . but he hurt me so bad . . . '

'He won't do that again,' Matt said grimly. The effort of talking was plainly draining the girl's strength and she was close to passing out. He had to get Devlin's whereabouts from her before that happened. 'Where are they?' Jenny's eyelids fluttered, her chin sagged against his hand. 'Jenny, I can't help Emmet unless I know where to find him.'

Jenny's head inched up, her distorted face mirroring her strain to remain conscious. 'P-promise you won't hurt Emmet,' she implored, her voice barely above a whisper.

'You got my word,' Matt said solemnly. He had no real grudge against the youth, it was Cole Devlin he wanted. He listened real hard while Jenny's trembling lips haltingly formed the words. Her voice rose and fell, out of control. Matt's eyes darted uneasily between Jenny and the door as her quavering voice grew in intensity.

'T-take right fork . . . up mountain south of town . . . go three miles . . . see cabin in clearing . . . ' With her last bit of strength she lifted her head from his hand, her body arching. 'Warn Emmet,' she said loudly. 'Tell

him it wasn't my fault. I didn't mean
to — ' She broke off with an abrupt
sigh and collapsed, her head lolling
over the chairback.

Matt placed his fingertips to her
throat and was relieved to feel her
beating pulse. Then he tensed at the
sound of heavy footsteps out in the
hall. The door flew open.

And in stepped Norton.

For an instant, the men froze, staring
in mutual surprise. Then Norton
rushed forward clawing out his pistol.
Simultaneously Matt snatched the lamp
from the floor and hurled it at Norton
as he flung himself sideways across the
room.

The lamp shattered against Norton's
upper chest, spraying his beard and face
with glass and kerosene. He screamed
hideously as his head and chest became
a solid blaze of fire. His wild shot
ploughed through the phonograph. He
dropped the Colt and, howling his
agony, wildly slapped at the flames.

Matt rolled to his feet and ran to

Norton. He grabbed the blindly reeling human torch by the back of his collar and charged him toward the window. With an explosion of glass, Norton's flaming body crashed headfirst through the window, taking the shade with him. His scream ended abruptly as he slammed into the hard dirt below. Matt stared down at Norton's limp, smouldering form, his broken neck twisted unnaturally. Then he heard a clamour of excited voices and footsteps pounding up the stairs from the saloon's main room.

Whirling from the window, Matt ran to Norton's pistol, grabbed it and bolted out the back door. As he rushed down the stairs to the waiting bay, which stamped and snorted, unsettled by Norton's nearby body, he heard the curious crowd enter Rath's quarters. No sooner did he jerk the reins free from the railing than several men appeared on the landing and yelled down at him. He ignored them, swung up in the saddle and rammed his heels into the horse's ribs. A bullet streaked after him as he turned into an intersecting alley.

Matt galloped along the alley and out on to a side street, scattering a band of possemen on foot who were heading toward the saloon. Startled, they hollered angry curses, but it was only after Matt was out of pistol range that somebody figured out he was the one they were hunting. Matt cut down another side street, then broke free of the town and rode like hell.

* * *

Sheriff Keeler stood in the middle of Main Street forming the bands of possemen into one large group, when a girl and the piano player from the Cut and Shoot Saloon urgently jostled through the crowd.

'Sheriff,' cried the red-haired girl, whom Keeler recognized as Maggie Thornton. 'Jenny Taylor's been beaten up something awful!'

Before Keeler could reply he was

distracted as Yance Boyne and a group of horsemen rode up. 'Sutton rode out headin' west,' the deputy shouted.

'Well, git after him,' Keeler snapped. Yance put his spurs to his horse and led the riders away. Keeler turned back to the others. 'Now the rest of you — '

'Sheriff, please!' interrupted Maggie.

'I ain't got time for no saloon quarrels,' Keeler said curtly. 'Send for Doc Burke, and I'll look into it when I git back.'

'But it's not what you think!' the redhead insisted.

McCann, the piano player, nodded. 'We found her all tied up in Jack Rath's private room.'

'Yeah?' Keeler said, frowning impatiently. Rath was a mean son of a bitch. He'd probably caught the girl holding back on him and was using her as an object lesson to the others.

'She keeps muttering something about Sutton's money,' continued McCann.

Keeler was now interested. He nodded and turned to the waiting group. 'Git your horses and meet me in front of the Cut and Shoot Saloon.' The men dispersed eagerly and Keeler accompanied Maggie and McCann to the saloon.

* * *

Matt Sutton reined in his horse on the crest of a hill and looked back toward the town. He saw the far off shapes of a posse tearing across the moonlit plain and toed the bay on down the hill. He came to a shallow stream and turned into it. If things were different he'd've led the posse all over the place and left them cussing in frustration. But Rath and his gunmen were already well on their way to Devlin's hide-out. This diversion wasn't much; still, it would slow the posse up a little. He followed the stream a'ways, came out on hard rocky ground, then changed direction and rode south toward the mountains.

A deep, bone-weary ache was setting in; lack of sleep dulled his mind.

There was no time to give in to his body's complaints: Cole Devlin was up in those mountains, and Matt was determined to take back both his woman and his money.

11

Diana lay watching the grotesque shadows cast by the flickering lantern playing upon the wall, trying to ignore Rose's presence, which wasn't easy. She could feel the woman's black eyes burning holes in her back and hear the maddeningly monotonous sound of her knife rubbing against her leather-clad leg, like a barber stropping a razor. The scraping kept her nerves on edge, as it was meant to, and probably wasn't that settling on Rose's nerves either. She sensed that the half-breed's hatred would soon boil over, and there wasn't anything she could do to prevent it. Even if she were free, she had never been in a fight in her life and would certainly be no match for the determined woman.

Would Matt find her in time, or would she be forced to accompany

Devlin to Mexico? The thought was distressing. But even more distressing was the thought that Rose might see to it that she never left here alive.

The front legs of Rose's chair came down on the floor with a bang, startling Diana from her thoughts. Then Rose approached, her high-heeled boots betraying her anger as they dug harshly into the wooden floor. Tensing inwardly, Diana quickly shut her eyes and feigned sleep. The footsteps halted beside the bunk. She could hear Rose's erratic breathing, feel the hatred emanating from her like a living thing, surrounding and suffocating her. Though her wildly pounding heartbeat threatened to give her away, Diana did her best to simulate the slow, regulated breathing of sleep.

'Cole's plannin' on takin' you with him, ain't he!'

Diana continued to sham sleep. Abruptly, strong slender fingers dug into her shoulder while others twined

177

and twisted into the hair of her scalp. Her eyes flew open, wide and fearful, and she was unable to suppress a half-cry as she was roughly jerked upright to a sitting position. Then her bound torso was turned at the waist so that she was staring into Rose's darkly scowling face. The woman's venomous eyes brought involuntary shivers and a horrible feeling in the pit of her stomach. Never before had Diana realized that someone could put so much hatred into a single stare.

'Dammit, I asked you a question!' Rose hissed, pressing her face closer. Diana hesitated, her mouth dry with fear. Rose's hand flashed, slapping, then backhanding Diana's face sharply. The sounds were loud in the stillness. She yanked her knife and placed its tip under Diana's chin, forcing her head back. 'Answer me, or I'll . . . '

'Rose . . . ' Diana began, choosing her words very carefully and striving to keep the fear from her voice, 'I don't want your man.'

'Well he wants you!' Rose removed the knife from under her rival's chin and lightly traced the outline of her face with its tip. 'Think he'd still want you if I cut you up a little?' The knife trailed down to the blonde's slender ivory neck. 'Or maybe I oughta just kill you?'

Feeling the sharp tip lingering on her jugular vein, Diana's desire for life overcame fear. She must make a sincere, determined effort to reason with her tormentor. 'Rose, would you give up Cole for fifty thousand dollars?' she asked, meeting her angry eyes evenly.

'I wouldn't give him up for anythin',' Rose snapped indignantly. 'He's my man!'

'Then you should understand how I feel about my man,' Diana said quietly. 'All I want to do is go back to Matt. Will you help me do that?'

Rose slowly lowered the knife and stepped back, studying her thoughtfully. 'Why should I?' she asked sullenly.

'There's nothing else for you to do. Hurting me will only turn Cole against you. And if I stay here he'll take me with him to Mexico.' Rose's anger appeared to be fading, replaced by concentrated thought. Encouraged, Diana swung her long legs over the side of the bunk and leaned forward, staring up into Rose's troubled face. 'Just let me get away and I'll be out of your life.'

'How do I know you won't send Matt Sutton after Cole and the money?' Rose asked suspiciously.

'I won't,' Diana promised. Then she realized that logic was more important than her mere word and added, 'Besides, you'll be gone before Matt could even get here.'

Rose shook her head. 'Emmet can't travel.'

'Matt isn't after him. Once I'm gone Cole will have to leave.' Rose pondered, glancing uneasily toward the locked door and listening to the faint murmur of the men beyond. Diana

180

waited tensely, eyeing the knife in Rose's hand.

'Cole would skin me alive if he knew I let you go.'

'Let's think of something so you won't be blamed.'

Rose looked Diana's securely tied figure up and down and shook her head. 'He'd never believe that you got loose and jumped me.'

Diana's hopes fell. She fidgeted, her fingers clenching and unclenching as she frantically sought an acceptable plan. Then something shifted beneath her stockinged toes and she looked down to see one of her discarded shoes. She glanced about and saw the other shoe lying at the foot of the bunk where Cole had tossed it. A plan began to form. It wasn't much, but it was something. She looked back up at Rose, whose brows were knitted in hard thought. 'Suppose you agreed to untie me . . . and while you were freeing my ankles I hit you with my shoe and knocked you unconscious.'

She nodded toward her shoe on the bunk.

Rose followed her gaze, then looked back at her thoughtfully. 'And if you was to do me up real good, so I couldn't holler or git loose, you could be long gone before anybody found out.'

'That's right. Will you do it, Rose?'

Rose shrugged and gave a prolonged sigh of resignation. 'It's better than doin' nothin'.' She turned Diana's body sideways, with her tied hands to the lamplight, and deftly began severing the taut ropes.

★ ★ ★

Each lost in his own thoughts, Cole and Jesse sat staring avariciously at the stacks of greenbacks piled beside the saddle-bags in the middle of the table. Finally, Devlin broke the silence. 'We'll cut this up 'fore we leave in the mornin',' he announced. 'You best go spell Shank 'fore he falls asleep out there.' Almost as though fondling a woman, he began replacing the money into the saddle-bags. Jesse stood but lingered, eyeing the bills. 'Somethin' wrong?'

Jesse shook his head, his eyes remaining on the bills. 'Just never seen that much money all together at one time.'

'It'll still be here when you git back.'

Jesse nodded and reluctantly took his eyes from the table. Cole continued his work until the door closed behind Jesse and his footsteps were heard moving away from the cabin. Then he sat back fingering a stack of bills. 'Sure be a shame to separate all this,' he mused aloud.

For almost two years, he'd waited, dreamed, and schemed to have this money, and now that it was his why should he split with the others? Sutton was no longer a threat, so they were all dead wood. It just didn't seem right to share with anybody he didn't need.

Besides, they'd only squander their share on women and whiskey within a year while he, on the other hand, had all sorts of good uses for the money. He was gonna be a big man in Mexico; there were lots of opportunities down there for a smart fella with money. He might just end up owning a whole big piece of the country.

* * *

Rose sat perched on the edge of the bunk while Diana, whose newly freed hands seemed all thumbs, tied her wrists and arms together behind her back. Both women's eyes darted back and forth to the chair wedged against the door as occasional stirrings were heard in the other room. 'If you can reach the barn without bein' seen,' Rose whispered, 'the rest is easy.' She paused, wriggled her arms to indicate the slack, and craned her neck back toward Diana. 'Tighter,' she demanded irritably. 'Cole can't suspect nothin'.'

Then she turned her head away so the white woman wouldn't see her wince and bite her lower lip as she felt the rope dig into her slim, bare arms, forcing her elbows to rub together.

'This path behind the barn?' Diana whispered, her lips almost touching Rose's ear.

'It's no more than a goat path,' Rose answered, 'but it winds around and comes out on the main trail, well past where they're standin' guard.' She watched impatiently as Diana knelt and began lashing her booted ankles together. 'Be sure to walk your horse a'ways first,' she cautioned, 'so they won't hear you leavin' down the trail.'

'I will,' Diana said, twining the long rope up Rose's slender, black leather-clad legs and knotting it above her knees. Then she sat back and looked up at Rose.

After a moment of critically testing her ropes Rose nodded her approval and said, 'Cole oughta believe me now.'

Diana untied the loose bandanna from about her neck, stood and leaned over to gag Rose. She hesitated, meeting her dark eyes, and said sincerely, 'Rose . . . thank you.'

'I'm doin' this for me,' Rose said without warmth.

Diana thrust the folded bandanna between Rose's teeth and tightly knotted the ends at the back of her neck. Then she scooped up her shoes and quietly hurried to the window on tiptoe. After several nervous moments of fumbling with the stubborn latch, the window swung inward with a raspy creaking of hinges. Diana froze and jerked her head toward the door. Rose sat stiffly on the bunk, her eyes, wide above her gag, were also tensely on the door.

No sound came from the other room.

Slowly the tension drained from the women's faces. Rose nodded urgently toward the window. Diana turned, dropped her shoes outside, then quietly climbed out after them. For a moment Rose stared at the open window. Then, sighing her relief, she awkwardly lay down on the bunk and waited for Cole to come in and find her.

Slipping on her shoes, cautiously Diana moved to a corner of the cabin and peered out. No one was seen lurking about. A shaft of light streamed through a side window in the front part of the cabin, bisecting the surrounding darkness. Hugging the shadowy wall, Diana crept forward on soundless feet. On reaching the window she paused and, very carefully, dared a glance inside.

His back partly to the window, Cole took a bottle of whiskey from a cupboard and threw a pondering glance toward the back room.

Diana's heartbeat staggered. No. Please. Don't let him go to the door!

Cole shrugged and turned away, his idea evidently discarded for the moment. He opened the bottle, took a deep swig, then ambled to the table and sat.

Hastily Diana drew back from the

window and composed her badly frayed nerves. She didn't know how long Devlin would stay put, but she sensed the bottle was to bolster him for another row with Rose over his visitation rights with the captive. Diana ducked under the window and hurried to the front corner of the cabin. Not seeing anyone about she started for the barn, trying to keep in the few shadows as she went.

* * *

His mind full of thoughts on how he was going to spend his share of the money, Shank shambled toward the cabin. It was then that he saw someone darting across the open space before the barn. He stopped short, standing in the shadows on the side of the trail and staring in disbelief.

It was Sutton's woman. How in hell did she get loose from Cole and Rose?

As he watched her pause in the doorway and cautiously glance about before disappearing into the barn, Shank grinned and ran his tongue over his dry, cracked lips. She was sure enough fair game now. There was nobody but him to stop her. His ugly grin horrible in the moonlight, the big man stalked toward the barn.

★ ★ ★

Diana stood staring at the horses saddled and tied before one of the stalls. There was no time to pick and choose; besides, she wasn't that familiar with horses. Several snorted and shied as she rushed forward, and she forced herself to slow to a walk. Speaking softly, she came up to the nearest horse and stroked its dusty coat. The animal calmed and she gave her attention to the knotted reins. Almost breaking a long fingernail in her haste, Diana unravelled the reins from a horizontal board across the stall. Petting and cooing, she led the horse away from the others, then halted, thrust a foot into a stirrup and started to mount.

'You ain't a-fixin' to run out on us now, are you?' asked a low, rumbling voice.

Startled, Diana froze, halfway into the saddle, and stared toward the doorway. Shank stood framed in the moonlight, blocking her way, a rifle dangling in one huge hand. Raw fear coursed the length of her willowy body.

'You know, Cole won't take kindly to that,' the giant taunted.

As he dropped his rifle and lumbered forward, Diana swung into the saddle, dug her heels into the horse's flanks and sent it bolting forward. But, instead of jumping out of the way as she'd hoped, Shank whipped off his hat, lowered his shaggy head and charged to meet the horse.

At the last moment the giant lunged aside, caught the reins and rammed a massive shoulder into the horse's forequarters. With a terrified scream, the animal sank heavily to its knees.

190

The jarring impact hurled Diana from the saddle and sent her rolling across the ground. She came to a halt inside an empty stall and lay stunned. Before the struggling horse could stand, Shank leaped over it and ran toward her.

Diana gained her feet, but she was too late. The big man grabbed her and they fell in a tangle. As they rolled about on the hay, their struggles taking them further into the stall, Shank pinned her beneath his near-crushing weight and slammed his mouth against hers in a harsh, demanding kiss, muffling the scream that rose from her throat. His foul whiskey breath was overpowering. Diana fought wildly, scratching, tugging at his hair, beating at his back and shoulders with her fists. She might as well have been an infant. Her arms were jerked back over her head, slim wrists imprisoned together in one huge hand. Then his other calloused hand roughly caressed her unwilling body while his mouth and beard left a wet, scratchy trail across her cheek and down her neck and bare shoulder.

Eyes squeezed tightly shut, Diana lay enduring his fondling. She knew the worst was yet to come — and there was nothing she could do to prevent it.

12

The back room door crashed open under the force of his savage kick, sending the wedged chair skidding across the floor as Cole Devlin burst inside. A sweeping glance told all: Rose gagged and all tied up on the bunk in the girl's place and the window standing wide open.

Face tight with rage, Cole's gaze swept back to Rose, who was squirming and making urgent, imploring sounds. He pointed an accusing finger. 'You damn, dumb half-breed bitch!' he snarled, staring flames of hatred. Recoiling from the whiplike intensity of his words, she shook her head and pitifully tried to offer incoherent excuses. There was no more time to waste on her, he had to get out to the barn and stop that commotion. Cole whirled and charged from the room.

Whimpering, Rose stared after Cole with hurt, tear-filled eyes. She'd made a tragic blunder in trying to help Sutton's woman. Sadly it confirmed what she'd feared: Cole no longer loved her. She lowered her face to the pillow and sobbed bitterly.

* * *

Jesse was about to enter the barn when Cole's harsh voice stopped him in his tracks. He turned and was surprised to see Cole. 'Who's in there?' he asked, frowning.

'Shank and the girl.'

Jesse stared in slack-jawed bewilderment. 'How'd she — '

'Never you mind,' Cole snapped. The girl's cry was heard over the sounds of agitated horses. Jesse eyed Cole questioningly. 'I'll 'tend to it,' Cole said, his eyes narrowing. 'Git back on guard.'

Jesse glanced at the cabin. 'Where's Rose?' The girl's cry came again, only to be cut short by a brutal slap. Cole ignored him and stalked into the barn. Jesse hesitated, deliberating, then concern for Rose drew him to the cabin.

Cole strode to the two moonlit figures frantically thrashing about inside the stall while the nearby horses whinnied and stamped, as though in disapproval. The sight of Shank's mouth and hands taking liberties that he had only dreamed of incensed Cole. 'Shank, git up from there!' he commanded, his voice low, harsh and trembling with rage.

Lost in his passion, the giant disregarded him. Cole's boot shot out and kicked viciously into his side. With a pained, startled grunt Shank tumbled off the girl and landed against the side of the stall.

'C'm 'ere, you!' Cole growled, leaning down and grabbing the confused girl's wrist. She offered no resistance as he yanked her up and started to drag her from the stall.

Shank sat up clutching his bruised ribs and fastened his gimlet eyes on Cole. Bellowing his rage, he lunged up, arms spread, huge hands grasping.

Cole shoved Diana away, sending her reeling, lopsided because she'd lost one shoe, further back into the stall, to sprawl in a corner. He spun to meet Shank's attack, but was an instant too slow. A brawny shoulder slammed into his belly, lifting him off his feet and bearing him along. As they smashed against the opposite side of the stall the rotting wood gave way and they landed in a heap inside the next stall. Locked together in unbridled fury, they rolled about belting, gouging, kicking and choking.

Dazedly Diana pushed herself up onto an elbow and nervously stared toward the battling men. She hoped the animals would kill each other. She scooted back and cowered in the corner as the men regained their feet and brought their raging contest nearer. She'd always hated the sight of men fighting. The blood, savagery and meaty, butcher-shop sound of blows never failed to turn her stomach. But she was the prize in this one and was unable to take her eyes away.

Cole's initial anger had now given way to an icy, sobering concentration. He'd known that one day Shank would challenge his authority, but had always hoped it would be settled with six-guns. Though he was putting up a good show he knew he was no match against the giant's bullish strength.

They closed, hammering with clenched fists, each seeking to end the fight with deadly, mauling blows. Cole ducked into a crouch, went in under Shank's roundhouse swing and drove a fist into his gut. The big man rocked back, then came at him again. Cole hit him between the eyes, to no effect.

As the huge arms started to encircle him, Cole pounded Shank's kidneys with both fists, but the panting bear of a man was wild-mean and oblivious to the punishing blows. The arms closed around him like a steel band, pinning his arms to his sides and lifting him off the ground. Cole urgently smashed his forehead into Shank's face, caving in his nose with a sickening crunch of bone and cartilage. Shank howled, loosened his crushing grip and Cole wriggled his arms free. He slapped his open palms sharply against Shank's ears, bringing another howl. Then he locked both hands together and brought them down on Shank's broken nose.

Yelling in mindless agony, Shank hurled Cole from him. Arms and legs flailing, Cole sailed backward and crashed to the ground inside the other stall. The force knocked the wind from his body and his vision was a blurred maze of red streaks and dots. Shank staggered about in his own blinding pain, then lumbered toward Cole's prone figure.

Diana had been so mesmerized by the violence before her that the thought of trying to escape while the men were distracted only now entered her mind.

Large eyes glued on the men, she eased herself up and, left foot standing on tiptoe to match her shod right foot, pressed against the side of the stall. Neither man's eyes were upon her as she began edging out of the stall. She glanced about for her other shoe, and noticed something glinting in the moonlight.

It was Cole's pistol.

She started forward cautiously.

Cole threw his hands up in front of his face, caught Shank's descending boot and savagely wrenched. Shank went sprawling backward into the other stall, forcing Diana to retreat from the pistol, and crashed to the ground. Cole sat up, grabbed a long broken board and lunged to his feet.

Shank got one foot under him and tried to launch himself up at Cole. Drawing back the board, Cole let him come all the way up before he swung. The board smacked against the side of Shank's head with a hollow *thonk* and broke in two. Shank spun around and fell to his knees, his back to Cole.

Murder in his face, Cole swung the now club-length board down on the middle of Shank's shaggy head. With a heavy, protracted sigh Shank toppled onto his back, legs bent under him, arms outflung, and lay still. Cole kicked him in the head for good measure, then stood over him, drawing ragged breaths through his open mouth.

For a moment, Diane stood in stunned horror from the scene she'd just witnessed. Then her desire to escape returned and she carefully moved to the pistol. Slowly her hand reached down for it.

Suddenly the club brushed her fingertips, struck the gun and sent it sliding out of her reach.

With an involuntary gasp, Diana stepped back in surprise, wringing her smarting hand, and turned to see Cole stumbling toward her. His hand closed on her arm before she could run and jerked her to him. She saw the anger in his face and wisely made no attempt to pull away.

'You give me any more trouble, woman,' he said between harsh breaths, 'and I'll knock the livin' hell outa you!' He sank to the ground, dragging Diana down beside him, and sat catching his breath. The black look left his face and he smiled, plopping a hand down on Diana's black-net stockinged thigh.

'That was some fight, huh?'

Diana was coldly silent.

★ ★ ★

Rose sat staring down with dull, unseeing eyes as Jesse picked at the final knot imprisoning her bound ankles. Her world had collapsed around her and, with the recapture of Sutton's woman, there was no hope of putting it back together. 'H-he called me a damn, dumb, half-breed bitch, Jesse,' she said, choking back a new flood of tears.

'He didn't mean it,' Jesse said quietly, not looking up from the stubborn knot. 'He was just riled.'

'You're always stickin' up for him,' Rose flared.

'You done wrong by helping her, Rose,' he said simply, without rebuke.

'I shoulda killed her instead!'

Jesse shrugged, pulled the rope free from Rose's ankles and tossed it aside. 'Killing don't always put an end to things, like some folks think.'

'Aw, let him keep her,' Rose cried in helpless frustration. 'I don't care no more!' She leapt up and, almost bowling Jesse over as she brushed past, ran to the door. Tears blinded her eyes and she hit one shoulder against the door frame. She staggered back with a startled yelp, clutched her aching shoulder, then kicked the offending frame and ran from the room.

His weathered, deep-lined face tight with thought, Jesse stared after Rose. He stood as her angry footsteps were heard racing across the front room and then the door banged open, striking against the wall. This was the moment he'd been waiting patiently for; he'd speak his piece to Rose and she'd be willing to listen. Unlike Cole, he'd be grateful to have her as his woman and he'd treat her right. With his share of the money they could get a small spread and settle down to raise cattle and kids. They'd have a good life.

* * *

They were into the mountains, riding up a narrow trail between two ragged boulders. Jack Rath's jaw was set in grim thought. Only a few more miles ahead was the end of his quest. He doubted that Jenny had lied, but it occurred to him that he should have brought her along anyway. Precious time would be wasted if he had to return to town and have Norton resume his methods of persuasion.

Rath pushed the thought from his mind and confidently told himself that the Devlin gang would be there. They wouldn't be expecting trouble, so it should be an easy matter to sneak up on the cabin. After they had been disposed of he would decide what to do with Diana Logan. It would be a shame to kill such a beauty, but he couldn't have her running to the sheriff and refuting his story about who gunned down the deputy. Matt Sutton must hang for that crime. Perhaps a stray bullet during the ensuing shoot-out would end his concern about the woman.

The trail climbed sharply and swiftly and the four riders reluctantly slowed their wheezing, sweating mounts. Rath cursed the delay, but knew they were getting close enough to use caution. Sound carried for miles in the mountains, and it wouldn't do to alert Devlin's bunch. He was counting on the element of surprise for a swift massacre.

★ ★ ★

Moonlight splashed Matt Sutton's tall, lean frame as his horse's hoofs ate up the distance separating them from the mountains, their serrated peaks looming against the night sky. The full moon worried him. There hadn't been much time to waste trying to throw the posse off his trail, and they'd be able to track him by the light, just as he was tracking Rath and his men, almost as easily as if it were day.

Rath's bunch had too much of a lead for him to overtake them, so the hope of slipping up to the cabin and taking out Diana before the two groups lit into each other was gone. All he could hope for was that the odds would be whittled some by the time he got there. Then, just maybe, he'd be able to take down those who were left standing. But the thought of Diana being caught in the middle of it heightened his concern. With Rath or Devlin she could expect the worst; he had to come through this alive for her sake.

When he reached the foot of the mountain, Matt reined in his panting horse and dismounted to let it rest.

A wary glance behind reassured him that the posse was not in sight. Still, it was only a matter of time before they'd come thundering across the flat, dry plain. He resisted the impulse to mount and ride on. To run his weary horse into the ground would serve no purpose, he'd only lose more time walking the rest of the way to Devlin's hide-out.

Matt studied the hoofprints leading up the trail. Rath's lead didn't appear to be as great as he'd thought. Gripping the reins, he began leading the wheezing bay up the mountain trail.

★ ★ ★

Limping behind on one shoe while trying unsuccessfully to slip on the other, Diana was dragged from the barn by Cole. They emerged just in time to see Rose's sobbing figure plunge into the brush at the edge of the clearing and Jesse hurry from the cabin after her. Cole halted and scowled after

Jesse. Diana seized the moment to put on her other shoe.

'Damn it to hell, Jesse,' Cole bawled, 'leave her be and git back out on the trail, like I tole you!' Jesse disappeared into the bushes without acknowledging him. 'Some folks just can't help makin' a fool of theirselves over women,' Cole muttered disgustedly. He gave Diana's wrist a yank and strode toward the cabin. Diana followed meekly.

On reaching the cabin door, Cole remembered his manners and herded Diana in ahead of him, none too gently. He shoved her down in a chair in front of the table. 'Now you set there and don't move a muscle,' he cautioned, then moved off. Diana let wisdom prevail and sat stock-still, hands primly folded in her lap, eyes on the bulging saddle-bags in the centre of the table. Cole returned and slapped another pair of saddle-bags before her. 'Rose's things oughta fit you,' he said, rummaging inside one flap. He pulled out a shirt and pair of leather pants.

'You can't ride all the way to Mexico dressed like you are.'

'I'm not — ' Diana began.

Cole's palm smacked the table top, cutting off her words and overturning the whiskey bottle near the saddle-bags with the money. 'I don't want ta hear no sass outa you,' he said, his voice quiet but hard as stone. From across the room, the wounded man stirred and moaned incoherently in his fevered sleep. Cole righted the bottle, disregarded the puddle on the table, then took a pair of low-cut moccasins from the pouch and tossed them on top of the shirt and pants. 'Now you git changed, I got things to do.'

Reluctantly Diana stood and picked up the clothes. Holding them to her breast, she turned and started for the back room.

'Where do you think you're goin'?' Cole asked.

Diana turned back to him. 'In there to change.'

'No more climbin' outa the window,'

Cole said, shaking his head. 'You'll change right here.'

'I won't!' Diana cried. Feet planted apart, arms folded across her breasts, she stood defiantly as Cole shrugged and approached with an air of tolerant amusement. He stopped before her and, undaunted by her frosty gaze, flashed his white teeth in a broad smile.

Abruptly, his pleasant manner vanished and his hand lashed out with blurring speed. The back-handed blow cracked loudly across Diana's cheek, sending her staggering back with a sharp cry of shocked pain. He caught her arm to keep her from falling and shoved his face before hers. She stared back at him with stunned eyes, a thin trickle of blood worming out of one corner of her bruised mouth.

'You gotta learn not to use them kinda words to me,' he said in his soft drawl. 'Now you peel and be quick about it, or I'll do it for you.' Their eyes met for a long instant.

209

Diana's lovely face was white and drawn, but the look in her eyes was hard and bitter. Then, hating it, she forced herself to nod submissively. Cole released her and stepped back, grinning happily.

Moving stiffly, Diana returned to the table, set the clothes down, then reached behind her and began to unhook her black costume. Cole ambled up, draped a leg over a corner of the table and sat watching her with a grin of anticipation. Summoning her iciest expression, Diana stared through him as though he did not exist and continued undressing.

★ ★ ★

Hoofbeats thundered deafeningly across the plain, leaving behind swirling, blinding clouds of dust. Grim-faced, Sheriff Keeler rode at the head of his posse. The story he'd heard from Jenny Taylor before leaving her in the capable hands of Doc Burke had cleared up the night's events to his satisfaction, and he was now determined to see that justice was done. Jack Rath was going to pay. Nobody killed one of his deputies and got away with it. Sutton, the Devlin gang and Rath and his lot could shoot it out over the money, then he'd swoop in and arrest those left standing. It would all be over tonight and Bedlow could return to being a nice, peaceful town. That ten per cent recovery fee would set him up good, no more risking his life facing down rowdies and outlaws. He could retire and leave that to younger men like Yance.

Keeler stared toward the distant mountains, ominous and brooding against the night sky, and wondered if Yance's posse was up there, or if Sutton had thrown them off his trail. It didn't matter, he had enough men with him, anyway. That whole outlaw bunch was up there waiting for him, and he was coming.

13

Jesse peered down over the top of a clump of bushes at Rose, bathed in a splash of moonlight, lying face down on the ground, head pillowed on her folded arms, sobbing pitifully. He watched sympathetically, touched by this very vulnerable side of her otherwise spitfire nature, and felt a pang of guilt that her sorrow was his good fortune. Steeling himself, he shoved through the bushes and went to her side. She appeared not to hear him.

He cleared his throat and said her name softly. 'Go 'way, Jesse . . . ' Rose said between sobs, not raising her head from her arms.

Jesse knelt beside her and, awkwardly but gently, took her shoulder, only to have her shrug his hand away. 'Rose, I only want to help,' he said earnestly.

She slowly quelled her racking sobs and turned her tear-stained face to look up at him. Jesse smiled and helped her sit up. For a time they sat silently, each waiting for the other to speak. Then Rose broke the awkward silence.

'Jesse . . . you like me?'

' 'Course, I do,' Jesse answered, lightly brushing the tears from her cheeks with one hand.

Rose managed a grateful smile, then said haltingly, 'Supposin' you had your own woman . . . ' Jesse nodded and, his breath tight in his chest, waited for her to continue. 'You'd treat her good, wouldn't you?' Rose asked. 'Say nice words to her . . . and let on how you really felt about her?'

'Every day of the week.'

Rose gazed into his smiling, weather-beaten face, her eyes wide and eager. 'Do you want me for your woman?'

Jesse could scarcely believe it. She had asked him, without him fumbling around for the right words on his own. 'What about Cole?' he enquired hesitantly.

'It's cut,' Rose said solemnly. 'I been tryin' to cling on to nothin' for some time now — and you know that.' Jesse remained silent. A wrong word might tip the scales back to Cole. 'But I'm done with him,' Rose stated, her moonlit face a bitter mask of resolve.

Jesse gave an inward sigh of relief; she'd finally come around to seeing him as the man he was. 'All right, Rose,' he said quietly, ' 'long as you're sure.' She answered with a determined nod. He placed his trembling hands on her shoulders and, gentle as if he was holding a newborn calf, drew her to him. She came against him desperately, her arms tightly encircling him. He kissed her as tenderly as he knew how and she responded eagerly.

★ ★ ★

Her exquisite face stony, arms limp at her sides, Diana stood naked, straight

214

and defiant, before Cole's blatant scrutiny. She felt her skin crawl as, grinning with open pleasure, he let his eyes slowly wander the length of her willowy, statuesque figure. After what seemed an eternity he nodded and expelled his breath in a long sigh.

'That little look oughta last me clean to Mexico.'

Diana shot him a swift glance of utter disdain and began to dress. She struggled into the skin-tight leather pants, then, trying to conceal her haste, picked up the cotton shirt. 'Wear it like Rose does,' Devlin said, reaching for the bottle on the table. He took a swig, saw her coolly questioning expression and explained. 'Roll the sleeves up high and tie the front ends together way above your waist, so you show a lotta skin.' Diana treated him to an icy stare but obeyed. Finished, she stood awaiting his approval. 'You sure do fill out them duds better than Rose,' he remarked.

Diana ignored the compliment. Taking

the moccasins from the table, she sat in the chair and started to put them on, then hesitated as Cole walked to a nearby wall peg and took down several coils of white clothes' line. Venom gleaming in her eyes, she watched him return.

'You can't be trusted here by yourself,' he said with a knowing smile.

She glared up at him, then dropped the moccasins to the floor and stuck her toes into them as he pulled her arms behind the chair. She sat unresisting while he deftly lashed her wrists together, winding the rope up above her elbows and drawing it tight. Diana squirmed a bit, but made no complaint — not that it would have done any good. He moved around in front of her and repeated the process on her ankles and knees.

Devlin stood and grinned down at her, then turned to the table. He stuffed her shoes and clothing into Rose's saddle-bags and slung them over his shoulder. 'I'll be back directly,' he announced. He opened a flap of the other bag, revealing the neat stacks of bills inside. 'You just sit tight and be thinkin' on how we're gonna spend all this money in Mexico.' He set the lantern closer, to illuminate the greenbacks, then grinned broadly and winked. 'Just you and me.'

Without a change of expression, Diana watched him leave, banging the door behind him. She waited until she could no longer hear his departing footsteps, then made an assault on her ropes. It didn't take long to learn that her frantic struggles were only tightening the knots.

★ ★ ★

Single file, Yance Boyne and his posse struggled up the twisting mountain trail on winded horses. Sutton's hasty manoeuvres had slowed them for a time, but they'd soon found his tracks again. There was no way he'd throw them off his trail now.

As far as the lanky deputy was concerned, Clark was always on the prod, and if Sutton hadn't done the deed somebody else sure would have sooner or later. His mouth twisted at one corner in a lopsided grin at the thought that both men had unwittingly done him a service.

Sheriff Keeler was more than a bit long in the tooth and would be retiring soon. Now, if he could bring in Sutton, dead or alive, before Keeler and his posse caught up, it would sure stand him in good stead with the town council. Then they'd think twice about sending for somebody from out of town to fill the sheriff's job. Yeah, he oughta be a shoo-in.

His mind filled with grand thoughts, Yance continued to set a gruelling pace and shouted for the others to keep up.

★ ★ ★

Hearing the dying echoes of two quick, distant gunshots, Rath and his men left their tired horses on the side of the trail and proceeded on foot. As there were no returning shots they dismissed the possibility that Sutton had arrived ahead of them and started a shoot-out. They hadn't gone far when they heard a single shot that seemed to come from the direction of the barn instead of the lighted cabin.

'If it ain't Sutton,' Rio said hoarsely, 'what in thunder is going on?'

'It's quite possibly a falling out of thieves over the money,' Rath ventured.

Spence grinned. 'That oughta make our job easier.'

They fell silent as a lean figure in black emerged from the barn leading two horses and headed toward the cabin. Though they were too far away to make out his features, the man obviously wasn't Matt Sutton. Then the distant sound of a lone rider coming up the trail claimed their attention.

'Ike, get back to the horses,' Rath

snapped, 'and stop whoever that is coming.' Ike nodded and hastily started back while Rath led the other two men toward the cabin.

They came upon the bodies of a man and woman shot while embracing and kissing. Rath was surprised by the outrage Rio and Spence expressed at the cowardly deed. Evidently, even these hardcases had some sense of fair play.

* * *

Diana stopped her useless struggles and looked toward the cabin door as Devlin entered wearing a sheepish grin. He walked to the table and stood looking at the bulging saddle-bags. 'Ain't it a shame what some folks'll do for money,' he commented in mock self-reproach.

'You killed them all,' Diana asked, stunned. 'Even Rose?'

Cole shrugged. 'It was the only merciful thing to do.' He sighed and shook his head at her appalled expression, then continued with disarming candour, 'Rose just couldn't live without me. And Jesse couldn't live without this money. Ole Shank woke up with a headache somethin' fierce, so I just had to put him outa his misery.'

Diana could only stare back at him in revulsion. Then she became aware of Emmet's moans and tensed as Devlin's gaze turned to him. Wide-eyed, scarcely breathing, she saw that his face had a hard set to it, his dark eyes malevolent. The muscles along his cheekbones quivered as he clenched and unclenched his jaws in thought. Then his face relaxed.

'Aw, hell, I didn't go to all the trouble of takin' a bullet outa him,' he said cheerfully, 'just to be puttin' another one in.'

The tension drained from Diana's face. Even though she had no reason to feel charitable toward Emmet Wade for his and Jenny Taylor's part in her abduction, she was relieved that Devlin hadn't killed him in front of her.

'Soon's I fill a grub sack we'll be on our way,' Cole said, chucking her under the chin and lifting her face to look up at him. 'How about showin' me how grateful you are to be my new woman?'

Before Diana could react he kissed her roughly. She squirmed and tried to turn her head aside. His long fingers twined in her hair, holding her head in place. Helplessly, she tolerated his kiss but didn't return it. Finally he ended her torment and broke the kiss.

Cole stepped back, wiped his mouth with a sleeve and grinned down at her. 'Still a mite icy, ain't you?' He winked. 'But you'll thaw out in Mexico.'

Seething, Diana sat proudly erect and contemptuously wiped her mouth against her shoulder. To her irritation, Cole only laughed good-naturedly and ambled to the shelves beside the stove, then began rooting through the canned goods.

With a slight sagging of her proud

shoulders, Diana looked to the cabin door and willed Matt to come for her. In only a matter of minutes she would be on her way to Mexico with this cold, insensitive killer.

★ ★ ★

On rounding a bend, Matt Sutton suddenly drew up his horse and stared warily at the four horses on the side of the trail, about thirty yards away.

They belonged to Jack Rath and his men.

Deep lines of tension carved his tight face. Were the four men slipping up on Devlin's gang, or was it all over and done with? If so, what about Diana? His guts twisted at the thought of her lying dead.

Forcing the grim image from his mind, Matt nudged the bay forward and sharply scanned the side of the trail. He was almost to the four horses when a man loomed up beside the last animal and fired a rifle over the top of its saddle. The slug screamed above Matt's left ear and took off his hat.

Gripping the pommel in his right hand, Matt dropped over the right side of the horse, keeping his foot in the stirrup, as it bolted up the trail. Unable to see him, the man stepped out on the trail and cocked another shell into his rifle. Jerking the pistol from his belt with his left hand, Matt leaned away from the horse and fired at the man's chest.

The force of the bullet kicked Ike back into the horse's hindquarters and the rifle jumped from his hands as it discharged into the air. Then he pitched forward, face down. Whinnying in fright, the four horses fled back down the trail.

Matt swung back into the saddle, transferred the pistol to his right hand and galloped on up the trail. The shots had alerted those ahead and there was now no chance for stealth. All he could do was ride up shooting and hope for the best.

At the sound of the first distant shot, Devlin dropped the heavy food sack to the floor and made for a front window. The second shot came as he got there. Every muscle in her supple body tense, Diana watched him cautiously peer out one side of the window and suddenly give a start.

'Looks like we got ourselves some company,' he informed her, recognizing the saloon keeper and his two gunhawks as they paused halfway across the open clearing and looked back in the direction of the shots.

'Matt?' Diana gasped, taking hope from his words.

'Maybe,' Cole said, turning from the window. 'But at the moment, it's your boss and a couple of his boys who are payin' us a call.' He strode to her side and lifted her out of the chair. 'You'll be safer on the floor when the shootin' starts.' He placed Diana down on her side, then stepped to the table and blew out the lamp. 'Ain't it always the way,' he said disgustedly. 'Trouble comes slippin' up on you when you least suspect it.' He sighed and added wistfully, 'I sure could use ole Jesse and Shank about now.'

Lying motionless, Diana watched Cole return to the window, draw his gun and smash the pane. She wondered if her fate would be any better with Jack Rath, once he got his hands on the money. The bark of Cole's six-gun drove all thoughts from her mind and she huddled lower on the floor.

Trying to avoid being caught in the open, Rath and his men broke into a run at the sound of breaking glass. Cole's bullet slammed through the left side of Spence's chest and sent him spinning to the ground, dead before he landed. Firing, Rath threw himself to the dirt and yanked his second pistol while Rio, fanning his six-gun, charged toward one side of the cabin. The two horses in front reared in fright and bolted for the safety of the barn.

Cole ducked away from the window as a shard of flying glass nicked his cheek. His face sombre in the moonlight, he looked over at Diana writhing helplessly beside the table as bullets whined about inside the cabin. 'Gettin' awful hot in here, ain't it?' he remarked dryly.

Diana winced and glanced up as the lamp broke on the table and, leaking a trail of kerosene, rolled against the bags of money, where it continued to empty its contents, soaking the saddle-bags and dripping down over the edge of the table. Another wild shot shattered the whiskey bottle, which added its liquid to the spreading kerosene. Hearing kerosene dripping on her leather pant leg, she began wriggling frantically. As she arduously inched her body away from the table, she heard Emmet groaning and deliriously calling to Jenny from the darkness on the other side of the room. Then she flinched involuntarily as the roar of Cole's six-gun filled the room.

Bullets chewing up the ground around him, Rath reached Spence's body and flung himself down behind it. Using the corpse as cover, he began firing both guns at the cabin window to give distraction while Rio carefully edged along the front of the cabin.

Matt galloped into the clearing, sawed back on his reins and quickly surveyed the situation ahead. The flashes from only one gun inside the cabin meant the Devlin gang was in bad shape. Rath wasn't much better, he was down one gunman. Well, he'd deal with them first and then tackle the one in the cabin. Crouched low in the saddle, he kicked the bay forward.

Rio was the first to see him and snapped off a shot. Then Rath turned and started blazing away. Matt swung down on the opposite side of his horse, Indian-style, using its body as a shield, and fired under its neck.

The .44 slug turned Rio's face to bloody ruin and threw him back against the cabin wall. His lifeless trigger-finger firing several shots into the dirt, his body slowly slid down the wall leaving a wide red trail and crumpled in a heap.

One of Rath's shots whipped a tuft of hair from the bay's mane. A second shot creased its skull and the horse started to go down. Matt hurled himself away to keep from being pinned beneath it. The ground swelled, and dealt him a hard sickening blow that drove the wind out of him. Fighting a wave of dizziness, he rolled with the fall.

Rath rose to his knees and started to take aim. The bay lurched to its feet between them, forcing him to hold his fire. The few seconds' delay gave Matt time to regain a clear head. He rolled in the opposite direction from the retreating horse and Rath's bullet kicked up a shower of dirt in the spot where he had lain. Matt brought up his pistol and fired.

Rath's chest exploded blood as the round tore through flesh and bone and pierced his heart. Both guns hurling lead into the air, he fell back heavily on top of Spence's body.

As Matt scrambled up, the gun inside the cabin cracked, sending a slug whining past his head. Firing rapidly, he charged the cabin. His bullets slammed into the window frame and drove the lone gunman back long enough for him to reach the side of the cabin. He was safe for the moment, but he'd emptied his gun.

'Thanks for savin' me the bother of killin' them two, Matt,' Cole called from the cabin in great good humour.

'Killing you is something I've reserved for myself, Cole,' Matt called back. Crouching low, he quietly made his way under the other window to Rio's side. He pried the gun from Rio's death grip and hastily began reloading it with cartridges from the dead man's gunbelt.

'Seein' how I got your money and your gal,' Cole called mockingly, 'I don't rightly blame you for bein' riled.' He laughed throatily. 'You want 'em back, come on in here and try to take 'em.'

'Matt, don't!' Diana's voice cried. 'He's — '

Matt stopped his work, a cartridge slipping between his fingers, and strained to hear sounds inside the cabin. After a tense moment Cole's voice called reassuringly, 'She ain't hurt none, Matt. I just stuck somethin' in her mouth to keep her from tellin' secrets.'

Matt finished reloading, tucked the six-gun in his belt and gathered two large rocks. He heaved the first at the cabin door and jumped aside. Instantly Cole's Colt cracked, sending two slugs splintering through the wood. Drawing his pistol, Matt hurled the second rock through the unbroken window on the other side of the door. Then, as the glass shattered, bringing gunfire, he rushed the door. It burst open under the weight of his shoulder and he dove into the dark cabin.

14

Matt hurled himself to one side, out of the bright moonlight that followed him inside through the open doorway, and rolled into the blackness. A shot from the other side of the cabin smashed into the wood floor and hurled a mass of splinters after him, several embedding themselves in the back of his coat. Matt sat up and, pistol ready, listened intently for sounds as his eyes scanned the cabin.

The moonlight spilling in from the doorway sliced the room into two dark halves, each with a dimly lit area before the front windows. A dripping sound drew his eyes to a spot in the middle of the room just beyond the bisecting moonlight. Squinting into the darkness, he made out a form huddled on the floor and then recognized the shock of light hair.

Diana!

It took all of his will not to go to her. Clamping his jaws together so fiercely his teeth hurt, Matt grimly continued searching the blackness for Cole Devlin.

A sudden moan drew his attention to his side of the room. Whirling, Matt saw a dark figure feebly stirring on a bunk, and took him to be Jenny Taylor's Emmet, the youth in the bright yellow shirt who'd taken a bullet during the wild shooting at the stock pens. He relaxed, let his eyes sweep back to the other side of the room, and again fought back an impulse to go to Diana. She was safe for the moment, and he'd only get himself killed crossing that wide shaft of moonlight to reach her. All he could do was wait.

The monotonous dripping, either from a broken lamp or bottle, was setting his raw nerves on end. He hoped it was doing the same to Devlin. From what he recalled, Cole wasn't long on patience. Surely this cat and mouse game was getting to him too.

Then it happened.

A loose floorboard creaked loudly in the darkness beyond where Diana lay. Matt fired and rolled further into the room. Immediately a six-gun flashed across the room, briefly illuminating Cole Devlin's black-clad shape standing behind a table. The slug dug into the floor, barely missing Matt's boot and sending splinters flying in pursuit. Rolling to his knees, Matt fanned his six-gun. Devlin threw hot lead back at him.

Trembling fearfully, Diana jerked her knees up to her body and lowered her head as the gunshots roared like cannons inside the cabin. Desperately she prayed that Matt would come through unscathed.

Matt felt a bullet tug at his coat sleeve. Another whisked past his ear. Across the room he saw Cole stagger and slump toward the table. He continued fanning his gun, driving the bullets into Devlin like coffin nails.

Disbelief contorting his face, Cole Devlin clutched at the blood-spurting hole in the middle of his chest and realized that, incredible as it seemed, he was dying.

Dammit, this wasn't supposed to be in the cards. Not now, when he had everything!

Squinting through a red haze, he pitted his last ounce of strength against the agony dragging him down on to the table and squeezed off another round. The powder flash ignited the spilled kerosene and whiskey and sent a ficry trail racing along the table top, engulfing the shattered lamp and licking at the saddle-bags. But Cole felt a different heat as a searing lead slug ploughed into his side, shattering his ribs and smashing his lungs and heart apart. He collapsed on the edge of the table for a moment and then slowly sprawled backward, pulling it to the floor with him.

Lost in his rage, Matt continued squeezing the trigger even though the hammer repeatedly fell on empty chambers. Then he was jolted from his stupor as the flames spread to puddles of kerosene on the floor, and a tongue of fire licked toward Diana's helpless form. Tossing aside the empty gun, he leapt up and, shrugging out of his jacket, rushed to her.

Diana gave a muffled scream and frantically tried to shove herself away from the approaching flame. She was hindered by her ropes. The flame reached her and crawled along her kerosene-soaked leather pants. She felt the heat and was momentarily paralysed, staring in wide-eyed terror at the fire slowly eating through the leather.

Suddenly a coat was thrown over her legs. Strong hands seized her shoulders and dragged her away from the spreading flames. Then she was in the wide shaft of moonlight and Matt was kneeling beside her, his hands urgently patting the coat and smothering the fire. But the smoking cabin was a dry tinder-box. Other flames, fanned by the light breeze from the open doorway and broken windows, were advancing toward her moccasined feet. The coat fell away from her legs as Matt quickly gathered her into his arms and made for the door. Smoke and heat stung their eyes, invaded their nostrils. The gag hindered her breathing and kept the smoke in her throat.

Then they were out in the cool, fresh night air.

Matt stumbled a short distance from the cabin, sank to his knees and gently lowered Diana to the ground. He quickly checked her leg and was relieved to see the flame hadn't completely eaten through the charred leather. Hearing her cough, he turned and clawed at the knot holding the bandanna wedged between her lips.

As the cloth came free, Diana coughed the smoke from her lungs and gulped in the untainted air. Her large, tear-filled eyes focused on Matt.

She spoke his name and, with a sob of relief, thrust her trembling body into his arms, burying her face against the side of his neck.

Matt held Diana to him protectively and stroked her hair as he felt his throat tighten at the thought of how close he'd come to losing the woman he loved. Haltingly he spoke words of comfort and vowed they'd never again be separated. Diana slowly raised her smiling, tear-streaked face to his and he saw the love radiating from her large blue eyes. Their lips met tenderly and, for a long moment, Matt was oblivious to all but the feel of her soft lips and supple body. Then wispy fingers of smoke blew over them, and something urgently gnawed at his thoughts.

Matt abruptly broke the kiss, drew Diana back from him by her shoulders and exclaimed, 'The money!'

For a second she stared at him uncomprehendingly, then saw the grim desperation on his face. 'It . . . it's in the saddle-bags on the table . . . ' she stammered. Instantly Matt released her and was on his feet, charging back to the flaming cabin. 'Matt . . . no!' Diana called, shaking her head wildly and tugging at her bonds. But her words went unheeded and fearfully she watched him disappear inside the cabin.

On entering the room, Matt drew his kerchief up over his nose and rushed to his discarded coat. One arm was smouldering. He hastily stamped on it, then grabbed the collar and began swatting the flames right and left as he moved through the scorching heat toward the overturned table. Behind him Emmet's racking cough was heard on the other side of the room. To hell with him, the money was more important! Slapping at the flames with a vengeance, Matt continued on, eyes streaming from the smoke's acrid bite.

As he neared the table, a horrid stench filled the smoky air. It was the burning of human flesh! Peering over the table, Matt saw what, at first glance, looked like a burning log. He didn't need a second glance to know it was Cole Devlin's roasting remains. He only hoped his soul was also roasting in Hell . . .

Then he saw the saddle-bags off to one side, flames eating their way through the kerosene-soaked leather. He ran to the flaming bags and hastily wrapped them inside his coat. Coughing and fighting for breath, he started back through the path he'd cleared, which the stubborn flames were again trying to fill. As he neared the door he heard Emmet coughing and calling to Jenny above the crackling flames. He took another step forward and then paused reluctantly, remembering the battered blonde girl and the promise he'd made in exchange for directions to the cabin.

It was because of her that he now had both Diana and the money. Dammit, he owed her, even though she and Emmet were part of Devlin's bunch, but he'd never be able to live with himself if he broke his word.

Matt ran to the doorway, heaved the coat outside and then headed back into the flame-filled room.

★ ★ ★

Diana saw the smouldering coat fly out of the cabin and anxiously waited for Matt to follow. The coat hit the ground about a dozen yards from her and the glowing saddle-bags rolled free. She spared them only a brief glance and turned her attention back to the blazing cabin. As she stared intently, wondering what was keeping Matt, Diana was unaware that the light wind was stoking the charred saddle-bags' unextinguished sparks back to life.

★ ★ ★

Choking on smoke, Matt stumbled to the bunk and pulled Emmet to his feet. The youth slumped and started to fall.

Matt caught him, draped Emmet's arm about his shoulder and supported him back toward the doorway. The toes of Emmet's boots scuffed along the floor as Matt half-dragged, half-carried him. The steadily moving flames were spreading across the room, threatening to cut off their path. Eyes smarting, struggling for breath, Matt wound his way around the flames. The youth was dead weight; he might as well be carrying a grain sack. Still, he had no intention of abandoning him.

* * *

Abruptly Diana became aware of smoke, other than that from the cabin, and bits of burning paper spiralling through the air. She turned her head curiously and gasped at the sight before her.

The saddle-bags were now a mass of flames.

For several seconds Diana stared in blank wonder, watching the flaming bills curl into charred, worthless ashes. She had never really cared about the money, and wanted it only because Matt did. But now that it was actually in their possession after the hell the Devlin gang had put her through, she decided she wanted it very much.

With an urgent cry she thrashed at her ropes. The knots remained secure. Tears of frustration formed in her eyes as she sat helplessly watching $50,000 go up in smoke. Then the bodies of Jack Rath and his gunmen soberly reminded her of all those who had died over the money. She didn't consider herself superstitious, but perhaps this was for the best. So far, the stolen money had brought both her and Matt only grief.

Still, it *was* a terrible waste.

Knowing what the money meant to Matt, and that only he could save what was left, Diana desperately called to him. There was no reply. Ignoring the flaming scraps tumbling across the ground, sailing up into the air, she focused her attention on the blazing cabin as her concern grew.

Then her tension fled as she saw Matt reel through the doorway with Emmet, followed by a billowing cloud of grey-black smoke. After half a dozen steps, he sank to his knees, dragging Emmet down with him, hacking and knuckling his eyes. Diana's eyes darted from Matt to the remnants of the saddle-bags and then back. 'Matt,' she cried, 'the money!'

Matt slowly raised his head, squinted over at Diana, then followed her gaze to the saddle-bags and gave a start. Lunging to his feet, he staggered to his coat and used it to beat out the fire frantically, only to find the bags and their contents had been almost totally consumed. He went to his knees, urgently dug through the charred ruins. The scorched bills crumbled, trickled through his fingers.

'It's gone . . . ' he muttered, stunned by the enormity of this unexpected tragedy. 'The whole damn thing . . . It was all for nothing . . . ' He continued pawing through the ashes, vainly searching for unburned bills. How in hell did it happen? Why hadn't Diana put out the fire? He turned to her accusingly, saw she was still tied, and angrily cursed himself for rushing back into the cabin after the money without freeing her first. But then, he hadn't counted on rescuing Emmet into the bargain. He scowled over at the semi-conscious youth and damned his own soft-heartedness. Suddenly Diana's excited voice burst in on his gloomy thoughts.

'Matt, listen!'

The sound of hoofbeats reached him and he looked toward the trail. He'd forgotten about the posse. 'They're after me!' he shouted.

'There are horses in the barn!'

Matt scrambled to his feet, ran to Diana, scooped her up in his arms and headed for the barn as the drumming hoofbeats grew steadily louder.

Yance Boyne and his posse cautiously reined their horses at the edge of the clearing and surveyed the area ahead. The burning cabin lit up the clearing like day and showed four bodies sprawled about, one of them stirring. Then a running figure was seen making for the barn.

It was Sutton and he was carrying a girl in his arms.

Yance hollered for him to stop, but he kept right on going. Yance jerked his revolver and spurred his horse forward. The others came after him, whooping with excitement.

* * *

As Matt plunged into the barn, he stumbled over a rifle and then saw a hulking dead man sprawled in front of a stall across from where the horses stood. He also saw there was no back door. He was trapped. And the posse was about to come boiling in on top of him.

'Matt, leave me!' Diana urged, squirming in his arms as he carried her to the nearest stall. 'You can get away . . .'

'It's too late,' he gasped between breaths, and set her down inside the stall, hopefully out of harm's way. Then he whirled and ran back for the rifle.

Slugs whined, kicking up dirt around the gun, as Matt appeared in the doorway. Somehow he grabbed it and dove to the other side of the doorway, away from Diana's stall, without being hit. He brought the rifle to his shoulder and fired several rapid shots.

The bullets threw up a shower of dirt and debris in front of the posse, breaking their charge as the lead horses reared in fright. Their riders struggled to bring them under control, while those in the rear frantically sawed back on their reins to keep their mounts from colliding. Horses screamed, men cussed, and dust filled the air.

'The next ones won't miss!' Matt bawled, as things quieted down some.

'Give it up, Sutton,' Yance Boyne shouted back.

'I didn't kill that deputy,' Matt said flatly. 'Both Diana Logan and that wounded man out there can back me up. So can Jenny Taylor.'

'They can all testify at your trial. Now come on out!'

'How do I know I'll finish the ride back to town?'

'I'll see you do,' Yance promised.

'Yeah, sure,' Matt called sceptically, 'till we come to the first big tree.'

'Let's just smoke him out,' shouted an impatient voice. Several others eagerly agreed.

'Better keep 'em under control, Deputy,' Matt warned. 'My sights are trained on you.' He let that sink in, then continued, 'Now your men might take me, but you and a couple more sure won't be around to see it happen.'

'He's bluffing!' a big man behind Yance shouted, and started to dismount.

Matt's round sent Yance's hat sailing from his head. 'Damn you, Briggs, stay put!' the deputy snapped, his face suddenly going pale. 'You want ta git me killed?' The man stayed in his saddle. The others looked to the intimidated deputy and waited for his command.

Matt threw a glance across at Diana who was tensely peering out at him from around the side of the stall. 'That should hold 'em for a while,' he said reassuringly.

'Matt, there are too many,' she said, her exquisite features etched with concern.

'I'm going to hold out as long as I can,' he said solemnly. 'Maybe Sheriff Keeler will get here soon.' Keeping a sharp eye on the posse, Matt told Diana about finding Jenny Taylor, and the ruckus as he escaped from town. 'By now Keeler knows the whole story and he'll be coming for Rath and

Devlin. Our only chance is to wait for him.'

The posse was sounding ugly again. Matt gave them his full attention. He didn't want to kill any of the fools. He was in the clear and wanted to stay that way. But there might not be any choice if Keeler didn't hurry up. That deputy was too weak to keep a tight rein on the restless men much longer.

'Listen, Sutton,' Yance called, his voice a trifle unsteady. 'Send the girl out and let me hear her story.'

'Matt, don't,' Diana cried sharply, shaking her head.

'We'll both do our talking to Sheriff Keeler,' Matt called.

'You expect us to wait while somebody rides all the way back to town and fetches him?'

'I got a feeling he'll be along directly. Let's all stay calm till then and nobody'll get shot — that means you in particular, Deputy.'

The night was cool, but Yance Boyne felt the sweat running down his face as he stared at the unwavering rifle protruding from the barn. Sutton had backed him down and everybody knew it. By tomorrow so would the town council.

Presently horses were heard approaching on the trail. Heads turned and an expectant murmur went up from the men as Sheriff Keeler's sombre, black-clad figure rode into the fire-lit clearing at the head of his posse.

'We'll let the sheriff handle this,' Yance announced, in a feeble attempt to save face.

Spotting Keeler, Matt lowered his Winchester and grinned across at Diana. 'It's gonna be all right.' Relief was plain on her lovely face as she smiled back at him.

Then Keeler's stern voice called, 'Sutton . . . there ain't no charges against you. Now you and your gal git on out here and lemme listen to your side of things.'

Matt tossed out his rifle and called back, 'We'll be there in a minute,

Keeler.' Then he went to Diana, untied her, and they walked from the barn.

★ ★ ★

The morning sun was still low in the sky as Matt and Diana reached the base of the mountain and reined in their horses. For a long moment, Matt sat gazing stonily ahead in the direction of Bedlow. Then he gave a heavy sigh and broke the silence which had lasted since they'd started down the mountain.

'We got a bright future,' he said glumly. 'I'm out the money and you're out of a job.'

'There really isn't any reason to return to Bedlow, is there?' Diana said matter-of-factly.

Matt considered, then shrugged. 'No . . . I suppose not.'

Diana held her features tight, but was unable to repress the sparkle in her eyes. 'Then there's also nothing to keep us from going to California.'

Matt regarded her soberly. Then a

grin slowly broke the impassiveness of his lean face. 'Well, what are we waiting for?'

They turned their horses and began following the sun west toward California and a new life.

THE END

Other titles in the
Linford Western Library:

THE BOUNTYMEN

Tom Anson

Tom Quinlan headed a bunch of other bounty hunters to bring in the long-sought Dave Cull, who was not expected to be alone. That they would face difficulties was clear, but an added complication was the attitude of Quinlan's strong-minded woman, Belle. And suddenly, mixed up in the search for Cull, was the dangerous Arn Lazarus and his men. Hunters and hunted were soon embroiled in a deadly game whose outcome none could predict.

THE EARLY LYNCHING

Mark Bannerman

Young Rice Sheridan leaves behind his adoptive Comanche parents and finds work on the Double Star Ranch. Three years later, he and his boss, Seth Early, are ambushed by outlaws, and their leader, the formidable Vince Corby, brutally murders Early. Rice survives and reaches town. Pitched into a maelstrom of deception and treachery, Rice is nevertheless determined that nothing will prevent him from taking revenge on Corby. But he faces death at every turn . . .